Anonymous

Life's Masquerade

A Novel: Vol.III.

Anonymous

Life's Masquerade
A Novel: Vol.III.

ISBN/EAN: 9783337051907

Printed in Europe, USA, Canada, Australia, Japan

Cover: Foto ©Andreas Hilbeck / pixelio.de

More available books at **www.hansebooks.com**

LIFE'S MASQUERADE.

A Novel.

IN THREE VOLUMES.

VOL. III.

LONDON:
CHARLES W. WOOD, 13, TAVISTOCK ST., STRAND.
1867.

LONDON:
BRADBURY, EVANS, AND CO., PRINTERS, WHITEFRIARS.

CONTENTS.

BOOK IV.

CONTENTS.

LIFE'S MASQUERADE.

BOOK IV.

CHAPTER I.

MR. BROWN.

In a sufficiently respectable and well-known *quartier* in Paris there stood, and perhaps still stands, a tall, thin house, bearing upon its door the sign—"No. 2 *bis*." It was situated in a certain street, no less popular than the district to which it belongs, but which, as exactness is not so much a necessity with the novelist as perspicuity, I will content myself with calling the Rue Vincennes.

The *concierge* of No. 2 *bis*, a sturdy little Parisian, with a coal-black moustachio, probably with a view of rendering less weighty the liabilities of his rent, had parcelled his house off into a number of dwarf-like flats, proposing to let as many of them as he could at a sufficiently cheap rate. Had this project of M. Mascot met with the smile of public favour;—in other words, had M. Mascot succeeded in letting all these little flats which he had set apart for this purpose, (himself and his wife either sleeping in the attic, or, for the sake of variation, on a sofa in the kitchen), there can be no doubt but that he might have assumed to himself the character of a gentleman and an idler; not only paying his rent from the produce of his flats, but positively subsisting in comparative affluence upon the money that was left after the rent had been paid.

But Fate, who too frequently smiles when her smiles can be dispensed with, and frowns when each additional wrinkle expands into a weighty calamity, had decreed, with a certain malevolence, that this excellent design of M. Mascot should be rendered almost useless; since, although he had been to some slight expense in advertising his apartments, only one lodger had been secured for the six flats in M. Mascot's house.

This man was English. Of that there was no doubt whatever; but this was the only certainty that M. Mascot could attach to him. What his employment was; what his age; what his means; what his society, M. Mascot could not tell. People never thought of asking him, and he never cared to inquire. The lodger paid his rent with regularity, and M. Mascot was satisfied.

The name of this Englishman was Brown. He was an old man—over sixty years of age, wearing horn spectacles, a long white beard, a long thin nose, ancient eyes, a wrinkled forehead, and a bald head. His profession was evidently literature—if that at least can be called a profession in which there is so much starvation—as could be seen by his two rooms on the second story, which had, scattered about them, numbers of books, quantities of newspapers in many languages, old pens, old dried-up ink-bottles, fragments of manuscripts, and all the rest of the paraphernalia that go to make up a man of letters. In a word, Mr. Brown was the Paris correspondent of a minor London daily paper, and had been so for some years; but had chosen to shift his quarters from the house of a washer-woman in the east end of Paris to the residence of M. Mascot—who appeared to be a sort of vagrant hairdresser—in the west.

Whether M. Mascot was ignorant of the nature of his English tenant's employment, it is certain that to the inquiries of an inquisitive wife, who used to say, " But, Adolphe, say, what does this man do up-stairs all day long?" Adolphe would answer with a shrug, "*Mais puisque je te dis que ce n'est pas mon affaire !*" As, therefore, there was no chance of my reader gathering from M. Mascot any knowledge of Mr. Brown, I have thought it right to introduce him myself.

The habits of old Mr. Brown were simple to the last degree. He would rise at seven, envelope himself in a flannel dressing-gown, duck his head into a basin of cold water, and commence to write. At eight, a little French maid would tap at the door, and bring in a roll and a small cup of coffee. This was Mr. Brown's breakfast. But often did this morning meal find him immersed in a certain volume he was compiling, which he surveyed as a monument of his future immortality, and to which he devoted all the hours he could snatch from his insipid business of sending letters to London upon foreign matters in general, and Parisian scandal in particular; so that the coffee was often quite cold, when, rising with a start, he would first look at the cup and then at his watch, and say, "Ah! it is positively eleven o'clock."

Then he would go out, and remain away until four,—busying himself in collecting each particle of news as it floated about him; with which store he would return home, and empty it into foolscap pages, destined for the editor of his paper.

One day he was seated at his table, his horn spectacles on his nose, and peering hard at some erudite compilation in which he sought authority for what he was about to assert, when there came a tap at the door, and in walked M. Mascot.

"The *bonne* is out," said the little Frenchman, bowing himself into a variety of attitudes, " and monsieur will therefore understand the reason of this *my* intrusion. I hope I do not interrupt monsieur?"

"What is it?" asked Mr. Brown, laying his hand upon the book, and turning to his land-lord.

"A young man who has expressed himself anxious to see monsieur supplicated me to put this into monsieur's hand. Will monsieur permit me to offer it him?"

Mr. Brown held out his hand, and M. Mascot placed in it an envelope upon which a name was written.

"Didn't he leave any message, Monsieur Mascot?"

"He is down-stairs, waiting for monsieur's permission to approach him."

"Oh, show him up, pray. No apologies—don't mention it," said Mr. Brown, as M. Mascot commenced excusing himself, amidst a multitude of bows, for his unavoidable intrusion.

The Frenchman thanked him, and went down-stairs. In a few moments he returned, and tapping at the door, threw it open with much solemnity of manner, crying "Monsieur Frederique Villiams?"

Mr. Brown rose and bowed with much politeness to his visitor, in whom, in spite of the mispronunciation of the name by the Frenchman, the reader will doubtless perceive the little boy of a former part of this story.

But the little boy had expanded into the young man; and in the Frederick Williams that stood now before Mr. Brown the fact was sufficiently proclaimed by the budding moustache, the large intelligent eye, the finely-chiselled

nose, the mouth expressive of vigour and determination, and the chest and shoulders broad
and well made. He was not tall; and in this
point only did he not resemble his father. *Au
reste*, the likeness was remarkable : all Hamilton
was expressed in his features—the mother, the
Eveleen of the past having faded away with the
last traces of infantine beauty. Surely Nature
here played a pretty part! To the child she
gave the sweet expression of the mother : to the
man the determined, almost haughtily vigorous
look of the father.

"Do you not recognise me, Mr. Brown ? " he
said, as that gentleman, having offered him a
seat, stood watching him without the least token
of recognition.

Mr. Brown looked hard at him through his
spectacles, and scratched his head.

" The name is familiar to me, too," he mused
aloud ; " but I cannot say I remember your face.
The truth is, sir, I am growing old—my memory
is beginning to get treacherous : let that be my
apology for not remembering you at once."

"You can recollect the Smuggs', Mr. Brown,
can you not ? Charles Smuggs, the bookseller ? "

"Perfectly well, sir,—perfectly well. I only received a letter from Mr. Smuggs yesterday morning. And now—'pon my soul!—now that I come to look at you—why, of course, I have met you at their house, haven't I?"

"Many times, Mr. Brown; and many a jovial supper we've discussed together in their snug little back-parlour."

"Dear, dear!" cried Mr. Brown, "fancy my not remembering you! Bless my heart—why, of course, you are as familiar as possible to me now! Heigho! I am growing old, indeed! And what brings you to Paris, Mr. Williams? I thought you had made up your mind to stick at the bookselling business?"

Williams slightly blushed, and answered,—

"The truth is, I had I suppose too much of what sent poor Chatterton to his grave—' a ——, native, uncontrollable pride.' It seems to promise to accomplish for me precisely what it did for him. For I leave a comfortable position to come to a strange place, where I find myself all at once penniless and friendless."

Mr. Brown sat himself down and examined his young visitor with an inquisitive eye.

"I do not exactly understand you," he

observed. " What could have been your motive in coming to a city like Paris, unless you had prospects of some kind ? "

" You are quite right: it must seem hard to understand, but I think a few words will explain everything." He paused a little, and then with an anxious glance at his old companion, to divine perhaps his mood, he continued: " I know you will call it pride, or perhaps by a harder name; but much as I am indebted to Mr. Smuggs for his kindness, great as has been his hospitality— I might almost say his benevolence, there lately stole over me an invincible repugnance to the business in which I was engaged. My pride whispered to me that I was superior to it—that I was born for better things. And though I could adduce no better testimony than my own opinion to support this conclusion, I was resolved at last to act upon it, and one day acquainted Mr. Smuggs with my determination to leave his shop, and commence, if I could, in the world, a career more congenial to my feelings."

" Well ? " said Mr. Brown.

" You must know," continued Williams, " that I was left alone in the world at an age too remote for me to recollect. My first friend, after my experience of many enemies, was a gamekeeper, a connection of the Smuggs', who having kept me till poverty compelled him to keep me no longer, sent me to London as an apprentice to his relation, by whom I was received and treated with the greatest kindness. This, in a few words, is the history of my life."

"I don't envy your future biographer's materials," said Brown. "He'll want a little imagination, I believe, to inflate this minute narrative!" And the old gentleman laughed.

"Well, sir, I was too young to appreciate anything but kind treatment. The business of bookselling appeared to me to be as good as anything else; and it is only within the last few months that the conviction has been awakened in me, that there are callings, if not better, at least more suitable to my disposition."

"Well, sir, and you've left it?"

"Yes; and I'll tell you how, having told you why. I took a strange idea in my head, which lasted a good week, that I would enlist; for I conceived that the position of a private soldier was more honourable than that of an opulent trades-man. However, consideration determined me to dismiss this idea from my mind, and I set about anxiously revolving in my brain the best course that I, a friendless youngster, could adopt to succeed in the world. How many resolves came and went, were fixed upon and dismissed, I will not weary you by detailing. One day, however, I met at Mr. Smuggs' dinner-table a man who proved to be connected with the press. He talked of a new paper that he, together with some others, designed starting; and he asked Mr. Smuggs if he would recommend him somebody who would undertake the employment of a foreign correspondent—that is, at Paris. Mr. Smuggs, looking hard at me, said 'Yes, I think I can ; and, if I'm not mistaken, here's the very person to suit you.' The man, whose name was Thomson, looked at me, as I thought, with suspicion, evidently considering me too young for such an engagement. Mr. Smuggs divined his thoughts, for he said, 'Don't let his years tell against him ; for, believe me, he's far ahead of his age. He's an excellent scholar '—(thanks to Mr. Smuggs' books," said Williams, with a smile. " I am not a complete ignoramus)—' and I'll warrant you he will suit you admirably. He wants to leave me ; and you'll be doing me, personally, a great kindness by giving him a lift ! '

"The long and short of it was, Mr. Thomson engaged me; and having bade adieu to my good friend, I left London five days ago, carrying with me in my pocket a five-pound note, and your address; for Mr. Smuggs desired me to call upon you on my arrival. I wonder he didn't mention my name in his letter!"

"No, he said nothing about it. However, it was more upon business than anything else; merely requesting me to hunt him up some obsolete books and so forth."

"Well, sir, let me conclude. I took my lodgings in the Rue ——; spent the greater part of my money in providing myself with writing materials; and despatched a letter to Mr. Thomson, acquainting him with my arrival, my address, and soliciting him for orders to act. By return of post I received his reply, telling me that the whole affair was exploded—the paper was not to appear—the promoters having quarrelled, and refused to pay their subscriptions. You may imagine my feelings! I have been now two days in Paris, and I spent my last sixpence yesterday morning. I am without a friend, and ——"

"And what?"

"Without a home!"

Mr. Brown shook his head, and looked grave. "Remember Jacob's prophecy of Reuben: 'Unstable as water, thou shalt not excel.' Remember, too, one more homely maxim: 'A rolling stone gathers no moss.' You would have done better to have stuck to the Smuggs'!" And, leaving his seat, he went to the door and called "M. Mascot."

The young man noticed the action, and a frown for a moment darkened his forehead; it was the perfect frown of his father, Hamilton! He rose from his chair.

"Where are you going?" asked Mr. Brown.

"I presume you have called for the servant to show me out. I will save him the trouble by going down-stairs myself."

The old man looked at him for a moment with surprise.

"You wrong me!" he said in a low voice. "I wish to order you some breakfast; you must be hungry, for did you not tell me you spent your last sixpence yesterday morning?"

Williams grasped his hand, and raised it with emotion to his lips. "I am hasty!" he murmured. "A fool—I am young!—Can you forgive me?"

"Sit down, my boy," said Mr. Brown; "we will talk of forgiveness when the inner-man is refreshed."

Here M. Mascot entered, voluble with apologies for the lengthened absence of his servant. Mr. Brown ordered him to prepare breakfast for his young friend, and to cook, in addition to the coffee, a couple of eggs.

"And what do you propose doing?" asked Mr. Brown.

"I must work."

"I suppose so. But, why not return to the Smuggs'?"

Williams shook his head. "It would be impossible. Much as I esteem them, I could never submit to the feeling of contempt which my conduct cannot help provoking amongst them."

"That's what they call pride, again," said Mr. Brown. "I will not insult you by offering you advice; but will you take an old man's experience? One half of the actions which we are frightened will excite ridicule is never noticed. Believe me, our vanity attaches far more importance to our movements than they either deserve or are believed by others to possess. Society only inspects flagrant crimes;

the minuter foibles of our characters are blushed
for by ourselves alone. If all the world thought
like you men would not subsist together. The
consciousness of our physical deformity, or our
moral turpitude, would fright us from each other's
society. No man is better than his neighbour in
the broad scale. The murderer only perpetrates
at one blow what others are years in accomplish-
ing in minute strokes. Charge every man with
the aggregate of those small sins which he
occupies a lifetime in committing, and justice
would thirst for the extinction of the whole
human species. No, sir, never mind the contempt
of others when you have no contempt for yourself."

This sermon the old man delivered with much
pomp of gesticulation and frequency of grimace.
Williams who had listened to it with composure,
was about thanking him for his counsel, when he
was interrupted by the entrance of M. Mascot
with the breakfast. Whereupon, without more
ado, he fell to his worthy friend's cheer with such
heartiness of appetite, as he alone can feel who
has fasted four-and-twenty hours.

" Still," he cried, between his mouthfuls, " I
cannot return to the Smuggs'! Rather than

resume that occupation, I will turn sailor, or enlist in a foot-regiment."

"But what do you intend doing?"

Williams paused in the act of breaking his second egg, and looking up, said, "Frankly, Mr. Brown, I called upon you to solicit your assistance, either to give or procure me employment. Any work you like to put me to, I shall be only too willing to perform. I merely seek a shelter and a crust of bread for the present, to keep me alive until I can find something more substantial."

Mr. Brown, who had been eying, with apparent delight, the appetite his young friend evinced in his discussion of the meal before him, suddenly assumed a thoughtful look, and said, "You do not, I believe, require me to tell you what, I think, this room expresses—that I am poor?"

"Nor," said the young man, with unfeigned warmth, "do I need any further assurance than that expressed by your present conduct, to inform me that you are good!"

The irrelevancy of this speech with that which had preceded it was forgotten in the compliment. "Yet," observed Mr. Brown, who could not restrain a smile, " whatever may be the qualities of my heart, I am afraid they cannot alter the state of my purse. However, it is right to assist those who merit assistance, and such I believe you to be. As I am poor, so you must expect only a poor proposition. Do not let your pride be ruffled at what I am going to say; nothing is easier than to decline an offer, and forget it."

" Speak it. Whatever may be my feelings, be assured of my gratitude."

" You have observed," said Mr. Brown, " that my occupations are wholly of a literary kind; this my books and papers have of course told you. But I wish you to understand, that by literature, I do not mean those occasional dips which are taken by some men as they take baths—as their inclination suggests or prompts them; but a severe, stern, sixteen, sometimes twenty hours' continuous labour, unremitted save for the five minutes' meal. Now, if I had my way, such would be my life; but, unfortunately for me, want compels me to pursue a routine utterly inimical to my feelings. Instead of wholly devoting myself to such congenial labour as that, for instance," pointing to a manuscript that lay upon the table, " I am compelled to gad about this huge city; or worse, to wade through long columns of newspaper literature, merely to pick up something worth saying in my Paris correspondence. Hence, I have barely any time for myself; and that time is rendered almost useless by the cares of my other duties. You understand."

"Perfectly."

"Very well. Now I will tell you what I am going to propose. Unquestionably, as a well-educated man, you would be of immense service to me. Frequently you might take my place and listen to the talk of the *cafés*, ay, and, perhaps, in time, write my letters to London. When fatigued with long-continued writing, you might take my place, and serve me as an amanuensis or copyist. Indeed, I perceive your value in a thousand ways; and, therefore, if you will agree to remain with me to execute such duties as I may suggest, I will provide you with a room in this house, with your meals, with whatever little comforts I can afford, and give you besides, six francs fifty centimes a-week, which will enable you at any rate to purchase yourself a cigar. I am poor; or, believe me, my offer would be more liberal."

To one in Williams' position such a proposition was a perfect God-send. In a moment he found himself provided for ; snatched from positive privation, and placed in comparative comfort. Nor were those duties likely to be imposed at all uncongenial to him. Literature he had long thought to adopt as a profession. It was a field in which he knew ability must at length meet with success ; it was bounded by a constant future of promise, to attain which, the only difficulty was to provide for the present. Moreover, he saw the value of an intimacy with a man so experienced as Mr. Brown ; he had long recognised the profound truth of Dr. Johnson, that, " He who proposes to become an anthor must first be a student ; " and by the side of Brown he knew that a constant study would be compelled.

It is needless, therefore, to say that he accepted this really kind-hearted old man's offer with gratitude. The matter was accordingly settled. M. Mascot was sent for, and to his inexpressible gratification, heard that another lodger was about to furnish himself with quarters in his house. Williams went at once and fetched his traps away from where he had formerly dwelt ; and thus it was that the son of Hamilton and Eveleen came to be the companion of Mr. Brown, and an occupant of No. 2, Rue Vincennes.

CHAPTER II.

ONE afternoon, when Williams had been some days in his new situation, the old gentleman requested him to go to a little *estaminet* some distance away, called the Café Victoire, and there, if possible, to enter into an acquaintance with an elderly man in white moustachios, and a ribbon on his breast; whom, he said, was acquainted with everything that occurred possible and impossible, " And who will provide you with the same the moment he comes to know you and drink with you.

" He generally comes in at four o'clock, and seats himself at a table near the door. He is good-tempered and amiable, but a little shy of making new acquaintances. Go, my boy, and try your luck; for I am anxious to discover the motives of Vicomte de ——'s last speech."

Williams hastened to comply with his old

friend's request; and, putting on his hat, made his way into the street. He had little difficulty in finding the *café* in question, having been directed thereto with unerring precision by Mr. Brown. On his arrival, however, he was disappointed at seeing nobody present who at all resembled his friend's description of the elderly man with the ribbon; but, observing a side-table near the door to be vacant, and concluding perhaps that its usual occupant had not yet arrived, he proceeded to seat himself by it, resolving to wait a little.

This *estaminet*, unworthily dignified by its proprietor with the name of *café*, was a low, long room, with a tiled floor, sanded, and furnished with a number of small tables projecting at regular intervals from the sides. At the further end of it stood a French billiard-table, around which, on this day in question, were assembled a few Frenchmen watching, with apparent interest, a game that was going on between two of their fraternity. At least so thought Williams, whose back being turned towards them, had contented himself with a rapid survey of them when he had entered; and, not perceiving him he sought, looked no more.

When Frenchmen play at billiards, however, he must have something more than even the phlegmatic nonchalance of a Dutchman, who can sit and listen to the tumult without occasionally turning his head and taking a look at the body of gesticulating men. Every moment after Williams had entered was increasing the volubility and excitement of the Frenchmen near the billiard-table; and, finding that there were as yet no signs of the appearance of the man he wanted, he determined to draw near, and inspect the cause of this excitement for himself.

The first thing that struck his eye, and which he silently wondered he had not noticed before, was the figure of a hunchback darting to and fro about the table, purple with excitement, but never opening his lips, except to utter an occasional "Pouff!" His arms were long, and in his right hand he grasped a billiard-cue, with which, ever and anon, he would strike his ball with a success that elicited loud cries from the standers-by, thereby denoting the cause of the tumult that had attracted Williams. His opponent was a little Frenchman, with thick eyebrows, and a great moustachio; the latter of which he very frequently stroked, whilst the former he was constantly contracting. Sometimes, when the hunchback would achieve a successful stroke with greater ingenuity than before, the Frenchman would shrug his shoulders until his ears were hidden, at the same time turning to a companion who dogged his footsteps behind him, and extending his hands with an emphatic *" Mais, c'est incroyable !"*

The appearance of this hunchback considerably interested Williams. That he was French, the absence of all vehement gesticulation sufficiently denied. But this fact seemed alone certain; for whether he was German, English, Italian, Spanish, or Portuguese, his aspect left it equally open to conjecture. It was not long, however, before he proclaimed his country.

" He is a brave player," exclaimed a looker-on, turning to his companion. " Jules, you will win your *petit-verre.*"

" And I my three cigars at ten centimes a-piece," exclaimed somebody else.

" Theophile, you'll be beaten !" exclaimed the man called Jules, addressing the hunchback's opponent.

" One is never beaten until one is !" replied Theophile, evidently angry. " However, had I known this gentleman's game, I should have been a little more careful at the commencement."

" Well, why don't you begin to be careful now; the game's a hundred, and I'm only eighty. You have time," said the hunchback, in barbarous French.

" Make him angry, and you'll put him off his game !" whispered Theophile's comrade, behind him.

" *Ah ciel !* he doesn't play with his head, he plays with his hands ;" answered Theophile.

"*Vive l'Angleterre !*" cried the hunchback, scoring six with a difficult but finely-played stroke.

" *Vive la France !*" shouted Theophile, striking a vigorous blow, which resulted in sending the ball clean off the table.

" *Ça ne va pas !* You musn't play like that!" muttered a man. "When you cry '*Vive la France,*' let it be at least associated with success."

" *C'est le diable !*" said Theophile to his friend; " he has bewitched my play ! Did you ever know such a game in your life as I am playing ? "

" Never !" was the consolatory reply.

At this moment the hunchback went in, and scored himself conqueror with a series of superb strokes that elicited from the watchers an uproarious cry of approbation ; and that even compelled Theophile, who flung down his cue in a huff, to mutter,

" Very well played, indeed ! "

The garçon having been paid by the loser for the use of the table, the Frenchmen walked away talking chaotically of what they had just witnessed, and repaired to a little side buffet, where their several debts in liquor and cigars were settled.

Williams returned to his table. As yet, however, the elderly man with the blue ribbon had not made his appearance.

He had not been long seated, before the hunchback—who had been left alone at the end of the apartment, strutted with a grotesque gait up to him, and staring him for a short while in the face, took a chair by his side.

" An Englishman, sir ? " he asked.

Williams nodded.

" I thought so : in fact I could have sworn it. I'll tell you why by-and-by. Did you know of what country I was ? "

"Not until I heard you cry 'Vive l'Angleterre!'"

"Aha! then you saw the game?"

"Yes."

"What do think of my play?" and the hunchback waited for his answer with a leer of triumph.

"Admirable!"

"These French fellows think themselves all
small Napoleons,—it doesn't matter in what.
However, we licked 'em at Trafalgar, and we
licked 'em at Waterloo; and every triumph we
make over 'em, never mind in what, I hold as
something added to the glory of England. Now
I consider my having beaten that little fellow at
this game of billiards, to be a miniature battle of
Waterloo. There isn't the slaughter, but there's
the same feeling of glory in having *licked* 'em!"

Williams eyed his deformed companion with a
smile. There was something exquisitely ridiculous in the pompous manner in which he had delivered himself of his sentiments.

"Your language won't do to be overheard here.
The French are a jealous people, and it is a
dangerous thing to beard them in their own
country with the boast of what they are anxious
to forget."

"That may be true. By-the-by, sir, what did you say your name was?"

"I am not aware of having mentioned it; but, since you are anxious to know, I will tell you. My name is Williams."

"Anything Williams?"

"No," answered Williams, slightly ruffled by the hunchback's manner; "Frederick Williams."

"Well, do you know, had you asked me to tell you your name, I would have said 'Frank Hamilton!'"

"Why?"

"Once I knew a man of that name, and you are the very image of him: that's all."

"Indeed! How many years ago was that?"

"'Pon my soul I forget! Never mind: what will you have to drink?"

"Thank you, I have had my *petit-verre* already, and that I only took in order that I might remain here. I seldom drink in the day."

"Nay, sir, you must join me in a glass, if only for the sake of drinking to my success at billiards."

After a little hesitation, Williams complied; and, the garçon being called, their wants were made known and supplied.

"You have asked me my name," said Williams, "pray what is yours?"

"Nathaniel Sloman."

"Oh! Have you been long in Paris?"

"No. And you?"

"A fortnight."

"Are you going home again?"

"Some of these days."

"What's your business?"

"Not to answer questions that concern no one but myself," Williams replied, fixing a cold eye on his companion.

Sloman was visibly disconcerted.

"You are quite right, and—damme! I could have sworn you were Hamilton at that moment!"

But Williams had turned his head away, annoyed by the familiar manner of the hunchback.

"Come," said Sloman, "our friendship is too young to quarrel. I am a stranger here, and so, I presume, you are. Here is my address. You must call upon me, and we will go about together, if you're willing."

Williams accepted the proffered card in silence, inwardly resolving to have nothing more to do with his companion when they parted. There was something in the expression of Sloman's face which Williams instinctively shrunk from, and he was not sorry when the door opened and he perceived the elderly man with the blue ribbon enter the room, and, finding his accustomed table occupied, seat himself at another that was vacant.

"I am anxious to make that gentleman's acquaintance," said he, indicating by a motion of his hand the individual in question; "you will therefore pardon me if—"

"That old fellow with the red in his button-hole?" inquired Sloman.

"Yes."

"Oh, I know him well. Come, I'll introduce you."

And Williams, not being able to find any excuse, rose and followed his companion to the table at which the old gentleman was seated.

"How do you do, M. Villiers?" said Sloman, nodding.

M. Villiers looked up.

"Ah, how do you do, Mr. Sloman?"

"Let me introduce you to a friend of mine, M. Villiers,—Mr. Frederick Williams."

The two gentlemen bowed, and Williams took a chair at the table.

"Well, I'm off!" exclaimed Sloman; "at least I am off, because, I suppose, you have something confidential to talk about. Two's company and three's none, you know. Mind you give me a look up when you can. Good-bye!" And, nodding familiarly to both gentlemen, he jerked himself out of the *estaminet*.

He had hardly gone, when M. Villiers, looking hard at Williams, said, "Have you known this man for long?"

Williams glanced at a clock over the door, and answered, "A quarter of an hour."

"No longer! Well, if you will take my advice, you will let the limits of this friendship remain where you have left them."

"Such, believe me, is my resolution. But let me ask you, do you know anything against him?"

M. Villiers shrugged his shoulders.

"Enough," he answered, "to tell you to be on your guard against him,—that is to say, if you have any money you desire to retain!"

"I have none: on the contrary, I am poor. But say, how do *you* know this man? He tells me he has only been in Paris a short time, unless, perhaps, you have met him elsewhere ? "

" No: my first acquaintance with him was here. I have known him only five days."

" Five days ! why he addressed you with the familiarity of a long intimacy."

" So do all his species. Now I will tell you where I first met him. In the Rue Antoine Sarbotière there stands a little house with a door painted brown, having its shutters closed all day long, and looking sombre and melancholy when all around it is gay. This house is kept by a man who was formerly a croupier at the Kürsaal in Homburg. Having saved some money he came to Paris, rented that little house with the brown door, and converted its lower rooms into a miniature kürsaal,—that is to say, in one room you will find a *roulette* table, and in another a table prepared for *rouge-et-noir*. Do you understand me ? "

" You mean, that in the Rue Antoine Sarbotière there is a gambling-house ? "

" Precisely. Well, as I happen to know Monsieur Karmadst, the ex-croupier and the proprietor, I sometimes step into his house to amuse myself,—not at play, but at watching the faces

of those assembled round the tables. Here, five
evenings ago, I met M. Sloman, your new
friend."

"Did he play?"

"Yes; and lost all he had in his pocket, some
forty francs, I believe. As I happened to be
standing next to him, he turned to me with a
rueful countenance, and exclaimed, 'Ah, it is
unfortunate that I have limited myself to two
Napoleons. Had I but another florin in my
pocket, I believe I should be successful.' Then,
after a pause, he said, 'Can you lend me a two-
franc piece?' I don't know what prompted me,
but amused, perhaps, by the grotesque form and
extraordinary features of the man, I put my hand
in my pocket and drew out my purse. 'But what
security will you give me—for you may lose it?'
He drew a light ring from his finger, and put it
into my hand. 'Hold that,' he said, 'until I
reclaim it.' I gave him the money, and before
ten minutes had elapsed, not only had he re-
covered his two Napoleons, but had actually
gained in addition eighty francs. I have met
him there once or twice since; but that is how
I first came to know him."

Williams had been listening to this account with

great interest. "Eighty francs!" he thought, "and in one night!" Then he remembered his six francs, ten sous a week, and sighed.

His companion seemed to divine his thoughts.

"If you will take my advice," he said, "you will shun this man's society. If once he can entrap you into that house you will be ruined."

" But how can poverty be ruined ? "

" But it may be kept poor. If once a love of gambling takes possession of you, look —tie a stone to your neck, and throw yourself in the Seine. You will be happier there."

" You speak, sir, as if you had had experience."

" No ; I profit from the experience of others. The eloquence of the flushed cheek, the dilated eye, the agonised expression, the despairing face, is quite enough for me. Men are content to be told that fire burns, without ascertaining the fact for themselves by thrusting their fingers into the flames."

" That is true. But, however," said Williams, thinking of the object of this visit, " to change the conversation, what news is there in the political world, or indeed in the social? That affair of the Countess —— seems to be exciting great attention."

He found the old gentleman very communicative and agreeable, as Mr. Brown had told him. Openly he avowed himself to be of no politics at all; but after awhile he secretly declared that in heart he was for the Restoration; though whether, as an old Royalist, he might not have meant Restitution, I will not venture to decide. The two gentlemen seemed mutually pleased with each other, and when they parted, M. Villiers expressed a hope that he might often have the pleasure of conversing with "*un jeune monsieur si agréable.*"

It will be found by the observer of human things, that coincidences, like misfortunes, rarely come singly; indeed, so frequently has this been found to prove the case, that it has been confidently accepted as a position, of which experience is for ever testing the value and confirming the truth. The rencontre between Sloman and the son of his enemy, Hamilton, was unquestionably a coincidence of a singular kind; and in what I am about to relate the reader will perceive another coincidence, to have succeeded that already detailed, no less curious in its circumstances than its predecessor.

On leaving the *estaminet*, Williams bent his footsteps in the direction of a certain stationer's shop, where he was in the habit of furnishing himself with writing materials. During the walk his mind was absorbed in reflecting over the conversation he had held with M. Villiers, dwelling more especially upon that part in which the worthy Frenchman had detailed to him the circumstance of the hunchback having, with a two-franc piece, regained his own money, besides a sum of eighty francs. To the young man on six francs, fifty centimes, a week, this money appeared prodigious; rendered even more so by the simple manner in which it had been acquired. A strange desire took possession of him to try his fortune in a similar way; a vision of untold wealth suddenly rose before his eyes: he saw himself all at once the possessor of thousands, scattering his money here and there with a reckless prodigality, envied by his friends, and adulated by the world. From the penniless young man, struggling for his bread, and dependent upon the resources of one hardly better off than himself, in a few moments' time he had promoted himself to the dazzling position of a millionnaire, returning in sovereigns each centime that had been given him by old Brown. But amidst his reverie, the still small voice of some inward whisper that had been subdued by the ardour of his first fancy, began now to prevail. It told him that the course his imagination had, for these few minutes, adopted, whether successful or unsuccessful, was wrong; that they were clouds floating above him rendered golden by the sun of his fancy, but which had only to be approached to become desolate, ominous, bleak. Indeed, this still small voice was proceeding to read him a very long lecture, had it not been interrupted by his approaching the stationer's shop, and abruptly entering it, for he was anxious to return to Mr. Brown, who was, doubtless, surprised at his long absence.

The shopkeeper was employed in serving a young girl, who was selecting from some of his wares that he had distributed before her on the counter. The tradesman looked up on Williams' entrance, and perceiving him to be a customer, cried, "*Dans un instant, monsieur*," and then begged him to be seated for a few seconds.

Williams did so, fixing his eyes at the same time on the profile of the young girl with a look of admiration. She was a brunette, but with the clearest of skins, almost transparent in the soft hectic that blushed upon her cheek. Her eyes, which she had turned upon Williams for a moment, were large and full, and of that darkness which is to the soul what the night is to the moon : revealing with more clearness the mellow radiance of the spirit that lay slumbering within. She was simply clothed, almost poorly; her dress being composed of some brown homely stuff, which she had looped up either out of economy or pride; economy to save the hem of the dress from trailing in the mud, or pride that she might display the little feet and delicate ankles that " mouse-like" crept in and out under her petticoats.

She was some little time suiting herself, sometimes going through a whole assortment of one kind of article before she could satisfy herself. This was the case, for instance, with a penholder. She wanted a penholder, and she told the man so. He brought down a box and showed her twenty different kinds at least; recommending them all in a strain of eulogy of which the energy with which it was delivered was proportioned to the price of the article. She was

apparently purchasing the whole furniture of a
desk; and at least ten minutes from the moment of the entrance of Williams elapsed ere her
purchase was concluded. The shopkeeper had
several times glanced at the young man; but
perceiving him to have his eyes fixed on the
girl, and displaying in his face no signs of impatience whatever, very reasonably concluded
that he was content, and therefore suffered him
to remain so.

"Shall I send these for you, mam'selle?"
asked the stationer.

"If you please."

"Where to, mam'selle?"

"Rue Colville, No. 15."

"What name, please?" asked the stationer,
scribbling the address down on a slate.

"Mademoiselle Rosalie Gautier."

The tradesman bowed, and the girl turned to
depart. But she suddenly paused; and, in a
frightened manner, retreated a step. Williams,
the moment she had pronounced her name, had
risen from his chair with a look of the most
profound amazement expressed in his face; his
two hands were raised in the attitude of astonishment, his cheeks were first of all white and

now red, and he stood exactly in the door-way.

This was the spectacle that had caused the young girl a momentary feeling of alarm.

The stationer, fearing perhaps that the young man meant some rudeness to the girl, had opened his lips to ask him his demands; but at that moment Williams cried,—

"Is it really possible that I have the pleasure of seeing before me Rosalie Gautier!"

He spoke in English; and the girl, after a moment's scrutiny, replied in the same language,—

"I have not really the pleasure of your acquaintance, sir?"

"Of course—of course! How can I expect you should? Seventeen, ay, eighteen years, effect marvellous changes. But I remember you, Rosalie. I remember that sweet little girl, at the hard-hearted Mr. Jerkins', who took pity upon a poor boy subjected to the tyranny of the old linen-drapering scoundrel."

A blush dyed the face of Rosalie; and she uttered an exclamation of surprise.

"And are *you* little Frederick Williams?" she asked.

"I was—but now I am big Frederick Williams."

"*O ciel!* is it possible? Dear, dear, how you have grown to be sure! Fancy our meeting like this! Oh, I am so glad to see you!" And the warm-hearted girl gave her hand to Williams; who, much to the astonishment and inward envy of the stationer, raised it to his lips, and imprinted upon it a warm kiss.

"Oh, won't papa be surprised too!" she continued, laughing with gladness. "Ah! this is certainly one of the most curious things that have ever happened to me in my life! Why, you were so *petit*—so little, when I left you! You were not taller than that!" and she stooped, and held her hand about fourteen inches from the floor.

"And you," he said, laughingly mimicking her measurement, " were not taller than that. If your surprise is great, what must mine be! Here I sat silently admiring a sweet girl, whose face kept me from growing impatient with the shopkeeper;—wondering what her name was?—what her age?—what, in short, everything about her! —and lo and behold! who should it turn out to be but my old, my good, my dear little friend

Rosalie Gautier!" And he spoke in such an accent of delight, that the little man behind the counter, whose knowledge of the English tongue was wholly limited to the pronunciation of the words "yes," and "rosbif," actually grinned with sympathy, and silently rubbed his hands together.

"But how did you recognise me?" asked Rosalie?"

"Why, by your name."

"Oh, of course. How lucky it was that I gave it: we might never have met."

She spoke so tenderly that the young man gave her an earnest glance, which she avoided by averting her eyes.

"But papa is waiting for me," she said. "I must go home. When shall you call?"

"Do you live far from here?"

"About three quarters of a mile."

"So far!"

"Yes: I had to come in this direction for something; and therefore called in at this shop on my way home."

"May I accompany you some part of the way to your house? I have so much to talk about."

"Oh, do come! do come!" she exclaimed. "And you must see papa;—and,—oh, yes, do come!"

"Can't I serve you with anything to-day, sir?" asked the stationer.

"No. I will call to-morrow."

"*Bon jour, monsieur! bon jour, mam'selle!*"

And, returning the polite salute, the two young people went into the street.

CHAPTER III.

Mr. Brown, M. Villiers, Sloman, the gambling-house in the Rue Antoine Sarbotière, were all forgotten by Williams now. He saw, knew, felt nothing but the sweet girl who walked by his side, whose charms he regarded with unfeigned admiration, and whose memory he cherished as the first one in the world from whom he had experienced the least kindness.

"Do you not remember this?" he exclaimed, putting his fingers down his neck, and extracting the little medal which was suspended round his throat.

"Oh, yes. And have you really worn it ever since?" she asked, with a slight blush.

"Ay, and intend doing so for ever. Shall I tell you, Mam'selle Gautier, why this medal possesses, apart from others no less cherished, one peculiar charm for me—a charm that invests it

with a sort of holiness, making me almost consider that so long as it reposes against my heart
I shall have a safeguard against all evil—an
amulet to mutely exorcise every fiend that dare
enter my thoughts?"

Rosalie stole a timid glance at him, and asked
why.

"Because," he answered, "it was given to me
by a little girl who was the first to teach me how
to pray to God."

"I remember," said Rosalie.

"I am sure you will not condemn me for
considering *that* the sweetest memory that is
attached to this little medal. I could name to
you a thousand other reasons why I love your
gift, but I choose to concentrate them into that
one sublime recollection. Ah! my young life
was dark until you rose like a star to render it
brilliant. Through long years of separation,
Mam'selle Gautier, I have never forgotten
you."

They walked on in silence for a short time,
both apparently lost in thought. At last Williams said,—

"Does your father still teach, Mam'selle
Gautier?"

She blushed as she answered, with visible embarrassment, "No."

"My recollection of him is so indistinct, that I can only just recall the fact that he was a teacher of languages, at Henley."

"He was poor then, Mr. Williams—and—and—poverty, you know, will incite men to pursue any course likely to lead them to wealth."

Williams looked at her earnestly. Her manner seemed distressed, and a constant blush, as of shame, suffused her features. He would not inquire the cause, though he felt curious to know it. At last he said,—

"I remember your father as a fine-looking man, with long white hair, and a dark moustachio : but not an elderly face. Has he changed much ? "

"Much, indeed."

"In appearance ? "

"And in character." This was spoken with a sigh.

After a pause he said : "I cannot understand you to mean that you attach any degree of ignominy to the profession of an instructor of languages, Mam'selle Gautier. An honourable man can suffer from no external defilement.

If he is to be degraded, it must be from within."

"Degraded—defiled! Oh, no, Mr. Williams. There was no ignominy in his profession at Henley. On the contrary, though a poor, it was an honourable calling. But now——"

She hesitated, and Williams came to the rescue.

" Has he left, then, his old profession ? "

" He has."

He saw that the subject was painful, and was anxious to change it. But she silenced a remark he was about to make by exclaiming,—

" Perhaps after all, you may not consider the calling he has adopted ignominious—but I am very sensitive: I do not like it. But I will tell you what he has become—a money-lender."

As she spoke, a bright blush again dyed her cheeks, and she kept her eyes studiously fixed on the ground. Williams remained silent: he knew not exactly what to say; and, misconstruing his silence, she continued rapidly,—

" But you must not blame him, Mr. Williams. He was a poor man, and his teaching only brought him a few francs a week. He had me to support, and—and—there is nothing *very* dishonourable in money-lending, is there ? "

" Frankly, *I* think no. But the prejudice of the world is against it: and it is not to be combated. The truth is, the calling might be made honourable; but so many Jews have employed themselves in this business, that their avariciousness and exorbitancy have rendered it notorious."

" But *you* do not think it dishonourable ? "

She laid a stress upon the you, and looked up at him gratefully. But even if he had, could he have said so ?

" No: the Jews have stigmatised it, but in the hands of a just man the business is honourable. Every tradesman in the country carries it on— but by different ways. The linendraper sells cloth and cotton; the butcher, meat; the grocer, candles; the baker, bread; the money-lender, money. Money is as much a commodity as bread, candles, or meat. There can be no dishonour in a man trafficking in it."

She was now looking at him with the same grateful expression in her eyes; the blush had passed away, and when he had ceased, she whispered, " Thank you."

" And you," he continued, " do you consider it dishonourable ?"

" I am hardly a judge, but I have thought it not right for anybody to prey upon the necessities of others. But, alas," she said, sighing deeply, " whether the calling be good or bad, it is not my father's adoption of it that I have to mourn alone; when he was poor he was generous, but now that he has become a little rich, he has grown mean—ah, I fear, a miser."

" You surprise me."

" After we left Henley my father came to settle in Paris. He was resolved first of all to pursue his former profession, of a teacher of languages, but no pupils came to him, and all the while we were living upon a little store which he had in one of the banks, and of which the remittances alone saved us from positive destitution. He grew gloomy and despondent, and whenever he looked at me he would sigh heavily, and sometimes a tear would dim his eyes. One day he told me that he was going to attempt a kind of business, which, he said, when he died would enable him to leave me a fortune. I didn't ask him what it was, nor did he tell me. He merely said he was going to draw all his money out of

the bank, and that he had taken a little office in the
Rue Colville, where we were for the future to live.
Well, we changed our abode, and day after day
my father used to sit in his office, and sometimes,
when passing to go in the street, I used to hear
the sound of men's voices talking, and the chink
of money, just as you hear it in a bank. Still I
suspected nothing, until one day in reading a
French paper my eye met an advertisement which
said—I forget exactly the words—that loans were
made to people on easy terms, but security, I
think it was called, was wanted; and after two or
three lines to that effect it ended with, ' apply to
Jean Gautier, 13, Rue Colville.' Ah, I remember
it also promised secresy. When I pointed this
out to my father he blushed a little, and said that
he could not bear to see me in want, and had
therefore undertaken what he knew to be a safe
and lucrative employment. I told him I would
sew, beg, do anything, if he would give it up—I
was so ashamed, Mr. Williams. But he called
me a silly, and said that he was making a fortune
for me to marry on. From that time I began to
notice a change in his character. First of all he
was rather generous, giving me money frequently,
and providing himself with many comforts.

Gradually, one by one, he deprived himself of these little necessaries, excusing himself by saying he was economising for my sake. At last he has grown—oh, I blush to tell you what; he eats little, he denies himself everything, and though his love for me prevents him treating me as he treats himself, I discover day by day an inclination to limit me both in food and money; and now it has come to such a pass that I am obliged to beg a whole week before he will advance me a few francs. In the meanwhile, he is growing rich."

This little narrative begun in English, her emotion had compelled her to continue in French. She communicated it with a trembling lip, and an eye from which the big tear was ready each moment to start. Williams listened with attention, until she had concluded, and then gently taking her hand, said, " You must not grieve over this, Mam'selle Gautier. When your father has acquired what he may consider a sufficiency, he will then resume his former character, and become once more the generous man my childish recollection pictures him to be."

He knew his consolation was poor. Young as he was he was keenly conscious that the love of money when once harboured, is the only human love that may be pronounced undeviatingly faithful to the object of its attachment. But still he spoke his sympathy with warmth, and for the moment thought to impart with it conviction.

But Rosalie mournfully shook her head. "Ah," she sighed, "there is no hope of that. Every day adds to the strength of this passion, and what he will become in the future I shudder to think. But "—she suddenly added, "you have told me nothing of yourself. Ah, my selfishness has engrossed for me the whole of our conversation. Or will you reserve your story for another time? you have a long way to walk back."

" How much further have you to go? "

" We are now in the Rue Brinvilliers; I have yet a walk of ten minutes."

" Well, I will, if you will allow me, accompany you to your house, as I am anxious to know where you live, that I may find you when I come to call. It will not occupy me ten minutes to acquaint you with the history of my life since I left Henley. Seventeen hours would easily comprise my actions for the last seventeen years."

But it *did* take him ten minutes to tell it, and more, for when they were arrived at the Rue Colville, they were compelled to take quite a round before Mr. Frederick's narrative could be concluded. Rosalie listened with profound attention to what he said, the expression of her face varying from sad to gay, according to the nature of the subject her companion was communicating. He certainly disguised nothing from her. He told her that he was poor, and that he might probably have been found dead of starvation by this time, but for the timely intervention of the honest Mr. Brown. He told her that his future was uncertain, that even his present was based upon the humours of an old man whom necessity might at any time deprive of the power to assist him. She listened to the last part of his story with emotion, and when he ceased he found her lost in reverie.

" But we have come again to your street," he exclaimed, "and there I see is No. 13. Well, I must bid you farewell now, indeed. But when shall we meet again ? "

She glanced at him with a faint blush, and answered, " Will you not call ? " then checking herself, she exclaimed, " but perhaps you had better not—that is—we might—" she paused, and appeared overwhelmed with confusion.

Williams very rightly divined that her first invitation, spontaneously spoken, had been checked by the consideration that her father's apartments were not such as she could desire a stranger to see. Evidently the poor girl was ashamed of her father.

" But you will let me come," he said, interpreting her silence by his reply, " we have not met for so many years; besides, your father knew me as an infant, there can be no question of formality between us."

She comprehended that he had divined her feelings, and she held her head down as she said, " If you come, then, Mr. Williams, you must take us as we are. The eccentricity of my father's character you will find everywhere painfully visible, and—and—I hope you will be rather inclined to pity than to ridicule."

He was holding her hand in his as she spoke, and he answered her by raising it to his lips.

" To-morrow evening, if you will permit me, I will call," said he, " and I shall hope to find you at home."

" You will find us both at home; we rarely are out after dark. Adieu." And with a quiet smile and a friendly bow she turned her back upon him, and advanced towards her house.

As he walked home an idea seemed to strike him. He felt in his pockets and producing the card that Sloman had given him, inspected the address. He uttered an exclamation of surprise, for he found that written in pencil, beneath the name, was—" 22, Rue Colville."

" That is singular," he said to himself, " for the house must be nearly opposite the Gautiers'. Well, the Rue Colville can boast its beauty and its beast, at any rate. No. 13, eh? I'll call to-morrow night for certain." Then after awhile he murmured, " I wonder where the Rue Antoine Sarbotière is?"

He was evidently thinking of the little house in it with the brown door, perhaps provoked thereto by Sloman's card, which he held in his hand. At all events his abstraction was very great as he walked home; so much so that twice he mistook one street for another, and even passed his own door some distance before he was aware that he *had* passed it.

On his entrance he discovered his old friend reclining on a low sofa, by the fireside, with a cloth round his head. He groaned as Williams opened the door, and placed his hand on his heart.

"I am very ill," he exclaimed. "What has detained you?"

Williams briefly told him that he had met a person whom he had known in years gone by; and then, with a look of anxiety, asked his friend what ailed him?

"I have a bad pain right across here," answered Mr. Brown, drawing his finger across his breast; "it seems as if my heart were affected: but I hope not—at least, not yet."

"Have you had any medical advice."

The old gentleman shook his head. "No," he answered; "I don't believe in it. I think I know what's the cause of it: I have a habit in writing of leaning my chest against the edge of the table; and that may have brought it on."

"You had better see a doctor; let me fetch you one.

"Do you want to ruin me?" asked Mr. Brown, first smiling, and then faintly groaning. "I shall be all right by to-morrow. Don't be alarmed," he continued, remarking Williams' anxious face, "I shan't go until I have finished *that,*" and he nodded in he direction of his manuscript that lay upon the table. "But sit down and tell me the news."

When Williams had done so, he placed himself at the table, and wrote for Mr. Brown, who dictated to him. The old gentleman was unquestionably ill, but he refused to see even the shadow of a doctor, affirming in an emphatic voice that they were all "humbugs," who aggravated the disease in order to enlarge their bills.

The young man went to bed that night with spirits rather depressed; but his melancholy was soon dispersed by the pleasant dreams that awaited the sealing of his eyes in sleep. One long-protracted vision of Rosalie was before him the whole night, smiling as only Rosalie could smile, and conversing as only Rosalie could converse.

The next morning discovered the old gentleman to be no better. He complained of a dull, lasting pain in his breast, especially in the regions of the heart: but as he ascribed it to the cause above stated, he was determined to have no doctor, convinced that time would cure that for nothing, which a physician would aggravate for money.

He was too unwell in the morning to write, and

from nine until one Williams was compelled to assume the position of an amanuensis, scribbling down all that fell from the lips of the old man, who, with a cloth still around his head, and his feet thrust into a pair of slippers, dictated to him amidst an occasional groan or sudden gasp of anguish, when the pain in his chest was more than usually acute. In vain Williams implored him to desert his book until he should have grown better; the old fellow with the persistency of age, and the ardour of a literary zealot, adhered to his duty, and continued dictating whilst Williams copied.

Thus the morning passed, and in the afternoon the young man sallied forth to pick up as he could such news as the *café*, or the gossip, could supply. The hunchback was not in the *estaminet* when he entered, nor did M. Villiers make his appearance there that day at all; and after an unprofitably-spent two hours Williams returned home.

It was now six o'clock, and at seven he had promised to be with Rosalie.

He took unusual pains to decorate himself previous to his departure, though had he been asked why, the possibility is he would not have been able to say; since it is certain that he would not have confessed to any other sentiment than that of friendship for Rosalie,—and a friendship not such as would have compelled him into any unusual elaborateness of dress or appearance. Not that the poor fellow, however, had much to dress in. Six francs ten sous a week, and of which the first payment had not yet fallen due, it must be confessed was a sum that by no means favoured the supposition of an extensive wardrobe. But happily for Williams, nature had provided him with that which unfortunately no tailor has yet attained the skill to supply: I mean, a well-shaped person and a handsome face; two gifts of which the advantages are, that whilst they can gain nothing from the tailors, the tailors gain almost everything from them.

"Are you going out?" asked Mr. Brown, who was reclining upon his little sofa.

"Yes; and I hope to find you better when I return."

"Thanks: I feel somewhat better this evening. I am anxious to get that chapter, which we commenced this morning, finished before to-morrow. If I am well enough I shall go on with it."

"Let me implore you to rest a little. Such

application can benefit nobody. You are injur-
ing your health by it, and I daresay doing no
good to the book. For who can write well in
pain?"

"Ay, but my boy, I am old. I have a task to
accomplish, and it must be performed in spite of
every obstacle of pain, of sickness, of sorrow.
Supposing I should die—it is likely,—what then
becomes of all my past labours? That unfinished
work would be valueless, and that future before
me, more cherished than my present, would be
blank—dark!"

He spoke with emotion, and pressed his hand
to his heart as he concluded.

A singular spectacle was this of an old man,
racked with pain, brought by age to the fair ex-
tremity of life, yet thirsting for that future and
earthly immortality which is chided in the young
as weak, which is reproved in the old as wicked.
He had been years occupied in the work upon
which he reposed his hope of a glory in the future
to which he well knew he would be insensible.
Night after night had this lonely old man bent
over those precious sheets, his pale and anxious
features illumined by the glare of a taper, medi-
tating, absorbed in his task, forgetful of all but

the mazes of that labyrinth of thought in which he, self-doomed, was wandering. How vague the incitement! — how wild, how fantastic the hope! What to him could be the future, bearing in its vast, impalpable profound the sublime promises of a higher civilization, of a nobler range of thought, of a grander sphere of action, of a loftier standard of excellence—to him, this fraction compared to an aggregate—this atom compared with a universe! What to him could be this future, beneath whose greatnesses he should be less than the weed that owns vitality—less than the insect unapparent to him in life!

But the manuscript was to be completed, and the old man was determined to take no heed of himself until it should be done.

"Fear not, my boy," he exclaimed to Williams, who stood lingeringly at the door, regarding him with an anxious expression, " my prayer has been that I may live to finish this work. I believe it will be granted. Farewell; have no fear for me."

The young man went down-stairs slowly and thoughtfully. Had he not promised Rosalie to spend the evening with her he would have remained at home with his aged companion; for from kindness on the one side, and a naturally affectionate disposition on the other, there had grown up in the young man's heart a love for the old, and in the old a tenderness for the young.

CHAPTER IV.

THOUGHTFULLY the young man had left the presence of Mr. Brown, and thoughtfully he made his way along the streets in the direction of the Rue Colville. As he approached his destination, however, he felt his heart grow lighter within him: pleasure at the prospect of being once again by the side of Rosalie, and of shaking by the hand a man who had known him such a long time ago, conspired to dissipate or subdue the growing depression of his feelings; and by the time he had arrived at No. 13 he felt comparatively gay and light-hearted.

Some little time elapsed before his summons was answered; then there came the shuffling of feet, of aged feet, along the passage, the creaking of some rusty bolts thrust back, and the door was cautiously opened. From the fact of its being dark inside as well as out, Williams, for the moment, was at a loss to know the sex of the person who stood in the doorway. But his doubts were soon set at rest by the person opening its mouth, and emitting therefrom accents of an unequivocally masculine kind.

"Who's this?" asked the man's voice.

"Is M. Gautier in?" inquired Williams.

"I am M. Gautier; who are you?"

Williams tried hard to catch a glimpse of the man's face, but the effort was useless, the light from a lamp some few feet down the street being such as to render the features visible as the sun is visible in a London fog, or the moon in a very hazy night. "Who are you?" re-demanded the man's voice in an agitated tone.

"I am Mr. Frederick Williams," was the reply.

"Frederick Williams! aha! come in! come in!" cried the man's voice in an altered accent; "my daughter Rosalie told me we were to expect you. Aha! why didn't you give me your name before?"

"To tell you the truth, M. Gautier," said Williams, passing into the hall, and standing there whilst the man bolted the door, "I wasn't quite sure who *you* were!"

"Aha!" evidently a favourite ejaculation of

M. Gautier's, Williams could see at once, and one that he pronounced shrilly, and with great rapidity; "Aha! well, Mr. Frederick, don't let's be standing talking in the darkness—there's plenty of light inside—plenty of light! This way." And groping his way in the direction of the sounds of M. Gautier's footsteps, Williams stumbled against the lowest stair of a flight, up which he laboriously and really painfully ascended.

When he arrived at the landing, M. Gautier pushed a door open, whence issued a stream of light, enabling Williams to follow his owl-like host into a little apartment lighted by two tallow candles, the smell of which was appreciable some time before the cause itself was seen.

Rosalie, who was seated in an arm-chair near a little fire, rose on their entrance and shook hands with Williams.

"I am afraid," she said, "you have found it rather troublesome to mount upstairs without a light. I begged papa to take one of these candles down, but he wouldn't."

"Tut, tut! certainly not. What for?" exclaimed M. Gautier; "and I'll tell you why I didn't—but first of all let's have a look at you,

Mr. Freddy! aha! You don't remember me, do you?"

"I remember your kindness to me, M. Gautier, perfectly well; but I cannot say that I can recall your face."

"Wonderful, wonderful! True, aha! all true! When I saw you last," said M. Gautier, "you were that height:" and as Rosalie had done, he stooped and held his hand a little distance from the ground. "Now look at you!" he continued, "ay, and look at me!"

There was really something to look at in M. Gautier: for a more singular face it would not have been easy to have met with. His hair, which had been white for upwards of thirty years, he had suffered to grow as long as it would; the result was it trailed some distance down his back, and lay in white folds upon his shoulders. This made him look older than he was; though the wrinkles about the eyes, and on the forehead, the sunken cheeks, the protruding under-jaw, the generally withered aspect of the nether man—his thin and bent legs being encased in tight brown stockings and knee-breeches made of some coarse stuff; sufficiently disclaimed all idea of his being young. He had shaved his moustache, which lent his face a long, conical appearance. His eyebrows were white, contrasting forcibly with the black, glittering, shrewd eyes they sheltered, and his forehead was thin, and receding, narrowing as it reached the top, and disappearing in a cloud of white hair. His age appeared from sixty to sixty-five years; but his singular appearance, united to the thin, worn lines about the face, expressive alike of care, of meanness, of cunning, perhaps of villany, gave him all the age of seventy or more.

This change in the man will appear more striking to the reader than it did to Williams, whose recollection of him was vague and uncertain. What really surprised him most was the strange appearance presented by the apartment into which he had been ushered. In a word, it was the abode of a miser. Everything was scanty, thin, and threadbare. Nothing was complete. There was not an article in the room that did not want either replacing or repairing. It was Poverty allied to Parsimony: Want united to Meanness!

The paper was greasy, stained, and torn. The ancient mirror over the mantelpiece was cracked and scarred. The little French clock had lost its hand and its pendulum. The red table-cloth was inky, oily, and full of holes. The carpet seemed thrice the age of the owner, and in place of a bell-rope, there was suspended by the side of the chimney-piece a piece of string, of which the only use seemed to cut the fingers of those venturesome enough to employ it.

But Williams did not dare to look about him. He felt, for he had observed, the eyes of Rosalie to be on him with a sad, almost imploring expression: watching him with a sensitiveness which the least perceptible token of contempt or ridicule would have bruised and wounded.

" Now, Mr. Freddy," said M. Gautier, looking about him for a seat, " my girl thinks it strange that I should have opened the door to you without taking a light with me. But I just want to show you the danger if I had. Supposing you had been a thief—I say, supposing! You smile; don't you think it possible ? Let me tell you, sir, this Paris of ours swarms with cut-throats and villains of the most terrible kind. Well, now, how was I to know that you weren't a cut-throat ? Aha! you see, I take no light, but quietly unbolt the door, peep out, and if you had been a thief, why, you wouldn't have seen me.

I could have shrieked for help whilst you were groping about the passage. Now, if I had held a light in my hand, you'd have found me out at once. Then, again, look at the waste of taking a candle to the door. Aha! my daughter forgot that! Look, she smiles; perhaps she thinks we are rich."

Rosalie was smiling; but it was a smile without mirth. Williams sighed to see a smile so sad, so bitter; expressive of such a sense of degradation on the mouth of so young a girl.

" I hope you were not fatigued after your walk last night," he said to her, in a low voice.

But low as it was the old man had bent forward at the first sound, eagerly listened, and had heard. " You weren't tired when you came in, were you ?" asked he.

Williams looked up with surprise. " Certainly," he thought, " this old fellow has marvellous ears."

" No, not at all," answered Rosalie. Then, turning to Williams, she begged him to excuse her for a moment, and rose from her chair.

" Where are you going to, Rosalie ?" cried M. Gautier, also getting up from his chair, and turning his face, with an anxious look, towards her.

She blushed and hesitated, and was about leaving the room without reply, when again he shrilly cried out, " Where are you going to ? "

She came back to the side of her father, and whispered something in his ear. The old gentleman shrugged up his shoulders, and answered, " But, perhaps he doesn't want any."

She blushed almost scarlet, and laid her finger significantly upon her mouth; but M. Gautier seemed to ignore the silent but expressive intimation, by continuing aloud, " At all events, you had better ask him."

Williams knew well he was the person referred to, indeed the subject of this little pantomime; but he looked another way, feigning to be intensely absorbed in the contemplation of a time-stained print that was suspended against the wall by the door.

" My daughter," said M. Gautier, " wants to make us some tea; she thinks you would like some. Now I never drink tea; Rosalie very seldom touches it. But then that needn't prevent you from having a cup—if you're thirsty."

Williams glanced at Rosalie. She had turned her back to him, evidently to conceal her face.

"Thank you," he said, " I have only recently had dinner, and——"

" Oh! Mr. Williams, you musn't mind what papa says," cried Rosalie, suddenly turning, and disclosing her face, crimson with confusion. " I always have tea ; papa knows it."

" *Comment!*" quoth M. Gautier, " never mind what papa says! What do you take your papa to be ?—a millionaire? *Ma foi!* I do believe you do! What would be the use of making tea for people who don't intend drinking it? It would be a waste! Wicked—ay, a downright piece of wickedness! Aha!"

Rosalie had given Williams a significant nod over her father's shoulder, and he thought the right interpretation was, " Well, M. Gautier, since you are good enough to offer me one, I *should* like a cup of tea." He was not mistaken, for when he had said this, Rosalie nodded again to him, this time with a smile.

" *Alors!*" exclaimed M. Gautier, bowing low, and extending both his hands, " you shall! *C'est une autre affaire!* Rosalie, my dear, go down and make us a cup of tea. Aha! but don't you think I was right, first of all to ascertain whether you wanted it before Rosalie made it?

Voyons! we are poor, Mr. Williams, very poor We are humble, and we detest with a great abhorrence all pretensions. If I had liked, nothing need have been said to you. Rosalie could have gone downstairs, made the tea, brought it up with much pomp, and so impressed you with an idea of wealth. But what for? We are poor, we are humble. You perceive it; we detest fuss, and waste. Aha!"

" You are quite right," said Williams, almost smiling, in spite of himself, at this singular being: " you are quite right. Prodigality I hold as a social crime, whereas self-denial is a great virtue."

" Bravo! You perfectly express my sentiments. Excess is surely a terrible wrong; and what is waste but excess? and excess, but prodigality?"

" Certainly. And so, M. Gautier, I hear that you have left your old profession of teaching?"

" Yes," answered M. Gautier, moving uneasily upon his chair, " I have."

" And taken up one of a totally different nature, M. Gautier?"

" Yes," repeated M. Gautier, still shifting himself uneasily, " I have."

" Well, I hope it pays you better than your pupils used to ? "

M. Gautier shrugged his shoulders. " Look!" he exclaimed, pointing, with his shoulders still up, and with both hands, around the room, " let all this answer you."

" But I thought the business of money-lending was singularly remunerative ? "

M. Gautier tried to throw into his face an expression of innocence, ill disguising, however, the marked cunning that was exhibited in his eyes. " So it is," he said, " providing you choose to forget that there are attached to it such things as bad debts."

" Ah ! I understand : you mean to say that it is an antidote that carries with it its own bane ? "

" Precisely. And besides, sir," he said, leaning forward and speaking in a kind of mysterious whisper, " there are such things as robbers in the world."

" True."

" I don't mean public, I mean private robbers. Men who go about in glazed boots and coloured cravats, and hats slightly tipped over the left or right eye. Men who even have handles to their names, sometimes comtes, sometimes vi-comtes, and sometimes," he added in a hoarse whisper, " dukes ! "

" I perfectly comprehend you. And so these are the men you suffer from ? "

M. Gautier winked. " Those are *the* robbers ! " he said. " You can defend yourself from a high-wayman, or a pickpocket, or any public robber— at least, you are so far prepared for them, that if they attack you, you are not astounded. But what are you to do against a fellow who speaks excellent French or English, who refers you to a noble mansion for a guarantee of respectability, who calls himself, and legitimately too, the Duc de this, or the Marquis de that, or the Vicomte de something else ? Hang it ! you'd fancy there would be honour there, at least. But no. It's quite the reverse : quite. Those men are the greatest scoundrels in the universe ! Look you— take my advice : never have any dealings with a man of what they call family. A long pedigree and a short conscience always go together. Rather trust a ploughman — his bread and cheese smack of honesty ; but don't touch those things called noblemen." And with another wink, M. Gautier pursed up his mouth and held his breath—perhaps in admiration of his own oratory.

At this moment Rosalie entered with the tea-tray. Williams darted forward to take it from her; but M. Gautier held him back. " She understands it!" he cried, "for mercy's sake don't you touch it. Ah, what a crash if you should let it fall." And, as if the crash had already taken place, he held up his hands and shuddered.

Rosalie's face was flushed with the exertion of mounting the stairs. She looked sweetly pretty as she stood by the little old table, endeavouring to make it appear respectable by ranging the cups and saucers methodically about it. The poor girl was evidently in a great state of mental distress, and it is to be doubted whether the occasional glance she darted at her irritating father, contained not sometimes more anger than reproach, and contempt than pity.

In spite of the constant uneasiness to which, by the delicacy of his position, he was subjected, Williams felt decidedly happy ; why, however, he could not exactly tell; but he fancied that Rosalie had something to do with it. Had it not been for her most visible embarrassment, he

would have unquestionably treated the conduct
of old Gautier as an excellent joke: laughed
heartily at an eccentricity that injured no one
but the possessor, and perhaps, with the spirits
of a young man, have improved the "lark" by
aggravating into torture the doubts and terrors
of this singular miser. Once he was about to
make a demand that he felt certain would have
frightened old Gautier into hysterics: but he
suddenly encountered the quiet eye of Rosalie,
and his heart smote him for even conceiving such
a design in her presence.

"What light did you burn downstairs, Rosalie?" asked M. Gautier, peering at her under
his white and shaggy eyebrows.

"Oh, papa, it doesn't matter now. Do you
take milk, Mr. Williams?" she asked.

"If you please."

M. Gautier sighed.

"And sugar?"

"Thank you, I take everything." Williams
had heard the sigh and could not resist this
little stroke.

M. Gautier heard and despaired. "Let me
see," he thought to himself: "two sous at least
for the milk; three centimes for the tea; three

lumps of sugar three centimes more : they're small lumps, that's a comfort! What did I say ? Milk ten centimes, sugar three, tea three. Sixteen centimes—three sous and a centime—ah, *ciel!* and for what ?"

Rosalie knew his thoughts well. Had she known Williams' equally well, the chances are she might not have felt so uneasy. But I doubt if she could have laughed with him. She loved her father, this girl, in spite of all his faults. He had been a good father in days gone by, to her, and she could not forget it. Now he was grown old, and infirm, and foolish, he was not to be despised. Once she was infirm and foolish, and he had cherished her! What is old age but infancy ? what is infancy but old age ? they are the meeting extremes—with this difference : one is to be cherished, the other to be loved. We adore the infant : we revere the old man. As she would not despise her father, she did not laugh at him : sometimes she was angry, but more often was she pitying.

The evening wore away : and by-and-by M. Gautier fell asleep in his chair. Then the two young people had it all their own way, and chatted to their hearts' content, discussing all manner of things ; and presently getting upon the subject of M. Gautier and his meanness, when, after a brief conversation, Rosalie found that Mr. Freddy after all did not consider her father with such contempt as she imagined. Indeed, she found his feelings to be of a nature totally opposite to contempt: far more akin to hers, which were, as I have said, pity. Her delight at this discovery was unbounded: and Williams, who could not account for her sudden smiles, ransacked his memory to see if he had said anything likely to have produced such an effect.

As I have a great, and I believe not an unreasonable, objection to chronicle love conversations, they all partaking of the same nature, and the dialogue of two lovers being quite sufficiently delineated if it be submitted to the imagination of the reader to suppose or to conceive, I will pass over the conversation that ensued between these two young people, making it my plea by briefly saying that it approached near enough to the level of all love-discussions to warrant my neglecting to insert it in these pages, as being useless to all except those it immediately concerned.

M. Gautier was awakened from his slumbers by Williams rising to bid adieu.

"Can you see your way down without a light?" said he.

"Oh, I think so," said Williams; "at any rate, if you'll kindly stand on the landing and show a light down so, I shall see."

"I can't do that," said M. Gautier, "because I've got to bolt the door after you."

"But won't you want a light to see how to do that yourself?" asked Williams.

"No," said M. Gautier; "I am used to the bolts in the dark: I can manage them better without a light."

"Oh, papa, take a light!" cried Rosalie.

"But suppose there should be a thief in the street, he could see right down the hall," said M. Gautier. "You forget that."

After some further discussion, he was at last induced to take a candle down with him to show his guest out: and bidding good-bye first to Rosalie upstairs, and then to the trembling old father down, Williams got into the street and made the best of his way home.

Before leaving the Rue Colville, however, he looked up at a house opposite, and perceived the shadow of a man delineated against the window-blind on the second story. "That's where the hunchback lives," he thought; "I wonder if that's his shadow." He stared, but it was too indistinct to remark the projection of a hump from the shadow, if hump there were.

On his arrival at the Rue Vincennes, he proceeded to his bedroom, which was on the storey above Mr. Brown's, without thinking of looking in on that gentleman on his way up, perhaps for fear of disturbing him, perhaps because his thoughts were too much occupied with other matters.

It was only ten o'clock, and Mr. Brown he knew to be in the habit of not going to bed until two, sometimes three, in the morning. For himself, however, he felt sleepy. He had taken a good deal of exercise that day, and was not at all disposed to be employed by the old gentleman for two or three hours in copying. Nevertheless, anxiety to know how the old man was, compelled him at last back again into the coat of which he had proceeded to divest himself; and, finally, opening the door, he took a candle in his hand and went downstairs,

On entering the old gentleman's room, he

observed him seated at the table, bent in the attitude of writing. There was a candle by his side, still alight, but burnt low in the socket; so much so that Williams wondered Mr. Brown had not taken the precaution to remove it so as to avoid the unpleasant smell that would necessarily follow its self-extinction.

He had removed the cloth from his head—apparently in a hurry, for it lay some distance from him in a heap, as if flung there. As his back was towards Williams, the face was not visible; but it rather surprised the young man that the noise of his entrance did not cause the writer to look up. Concluding that he was too absorbed in thought (he was evidently not writing) to hear anything, Williams approached on tiptoe, and peered over his shoulder. The old gentleman's left hand reposed upon a piece of white paper, whilst his right grasped a pen, the point of which had paused in the act of concluding a word. Beneath this paper lay the cherished manuscript upon which the writer had evidently been busily engaged before some thoughts, which he was apparently tracing now, had called him away from it. So completely natural, so full of life, was the attitude of the old man, that his perfect stillness, so long protracted, amazed, and presently began to alarm, Williams. Still hesitating to disturb him, for he knew how the least movement will interrupt or mar the delicate organisation of a train of thought, he stole softly round to the other side of the table, and, bending down, looked up into the old man's face.

The eyes were fixed and staring; there was an expression of keen agony upon the face; the muscles of the cheeks and brows were contracted, and knottily developed with appalling accuracy through the skin; the under jaw had fallen, and the open mouth lent an appearance to the face as if the old man was in the act of raising a loud shout.

With an exclamation of alarm, Williams returned to the side of his motionless companion, and, taking him by the arm, lightly shook him. Terrified by the non-resistance, by the want of elasticity in the limb that he had grasped, he again shook him—more violently than he intended, for the old man, swaying himself to and fro with a dead motion to the movements of Williams, suddenly seemed to lose his balance, and rolled sideways on the floor, still retaining the attitude of a seated man, his legs bent, his arms out as if writing, his form inclined forward, and his whole body set with the rigidity of a corpse.

For a moment Williams was too terrified to act; but his presence of mind suddenly returning, he rushed to the bell and pulled it violently; then darting to the side of the old man, raised and carried him to the sofa. The most appalling spectacle was the fixed attitude of the body. In vain he attempted to press the legs down straight, to smooth the arm by its side; they resisted his endeavours, as if the old man were determined to maintain in death his favourite attitude when on earth—the attitude of a man writing.

The loud summons soon brought M. Mascot to the room, followed by his wife, whom curiosity and fright had compelled to pursue the footsteps of her husband. On seeing the prostrate form of the old man on the sofa, apparently in convulsions, the Frenchman rushed to the side of Williams, who was bending over the body, and implored him to say what was the matter.

"Run for a doctor—quick!" cried Williams. "Mr. Brown is either dying or dead. Quick—pray!"

" *J'irai, Adolphe!* " exclaimed Madame Mascot, and instantly left the room.

" Ah, he is dead!" cried M. Mascot.

" He may not be," answered Williams; " perhaps this is a lethargy—a swoon—a fit; a thousand things—not death."

The Frenchman shrugged his shoulders. " Look at the face," he said; " only dead men wear such an expression."

" I will pour some brandy down his throat—it may revive him."

" He'll wake no more," answered M. Mascot; " *au moins*, on this side the grave," he added, with the devotion of a Catholic. " How did monsieur discover his friend?"

Williams briefly told him, and when his account was concluded, M. Mascot cried, " *Ah, voilà M. le Médecin!* "

At the same moment sounds of footsteps were heard outside, and the doctor entered, accompanied by Madame Mascot. He looked at the body in silence for a few moments, and then approaching it placed his hand upon its forehead, and next upon its wrist. Then turning to Williams, he said, " Your friend is dead, sir."

Williams bowed his head with a gesture full of sorrow.

" I thought so," said M. Mascot. " The expression on his face is that of a dead man."

" Yes," answered the doctor, " and the expression of a man who has died of apoplexy."

Williams told him that the deceased had for some time complained of a pain about the heart.

" Ah, well, I will go and send a *Sœur de Charité* here, to watch by the body. To-morrow we will hold a post-mortem examination. Meanwhile, messieurs, *bon soir* ; madame, *à vous.*" And tapping his snuff-box and bowing with much politeness all around, the doctor left the room.

Had the corpse worn better clothes, its friend a wealthier aspect, or the room a more handsome appearance, the chances are the doctor's departure might not have been so abrupt.

Before leaving the room of death, Williams cast his eyes around, with a view of collecting the poor old man's papers, so as to secrete them from the gaze of the curious or the stranger. Some connection or relation the old man might have to whom the fruits of his incessant toil, as rendered apparent in the manuscripts, &c., piled up in drawers, or open on the table, might be useful. He approached the chair upon which the dead man had so lately been seated, and noticed upon it a piece of paper, which he took up and read. It was the paper upon which Mr. Brown had been employed writing, and it was already more than two-thirds occupied. Perceiving his own name standing at the head, Williams trimmed the light that had been left by M. Mascot, and seating him-self by it proceeded to read. It was short, for the old man wrote a large, rambling hand: and this is what it said,—

"MY DEAR WILLIAMS,

"One of those strange presentiments which, like voices from the future, sometimes speak to the heart of man, is upon me. Its nature I cannot define, but its presence I can feel. This I frankly confess to you, and let the confession rather attest my candour than my weakness, for what man willingly owns that he is superstitious?

"If I should die—I will be plain and short with you—this is what I wish you to do with me. Bury me in the cemetery of Père-la-Chaise, and have erected over me a simple stone, with these words :—

" ' JOHANNIS BROWN,

Obiit ——

Anno Domini ——

An. Ætat. Suæ ——

" ' I returned, and saw under the sun, that the race is not to the swift, nor the battle to the strong, neither yet bread to the wise, nor yet riches to men of understanding, nor yet favour to men of skill; but time and chance happeneth to them all.—*Eccl.* ix. 11.'

" You must fill up the dates. I will not weary you by informing you of my meaning in this passage from the preacher. It will be intelligible to my spirit who shall perhaps stand by and mournfully read it.

" I have no relations—no friends. I therefore leave you all that I cannot take with me. If I die before my MS. is completed, burn it, and in its ashes you will perhaps discern the hopes of a man " (here there were some blots, and the writing was illegible) .... " out of what I leave you. My books you can sell. You will find some money in my desk. My heart begins to th . . . ."

Here the letter had ended, and with it the life of the old man. The *Sœur de Charité*, in her sombre apparel, entering, Williams betook himself to his bed-room with a slow and sad step. His heart was full, and it wanted but the kindly accent of sympathy to bring the tears to his eyes. His only friend had gone from him now. What should he do? The Future was dark before him. It is true the presence of Rosalie threw around her a soft and tender light, but all else was bleak and desolate. There was, however, one hope; he would write to the editor of the paper upon which his deceased friend had been employed, acquainting him with his death, and request to be permitted to supply the place of a man whom in life he had frequently assisted, and whose letters were often his own composition.

This letter he sat down and wrote at once, and when concluded, sallied forth and put it in the post. Then returning, he retired to his apartment, and asking God to grant him His assistance, and to have mercy upon the soul of his old friend who lay dead beneath him, he slipped into bed, and was soon asleep.

CHAPTER V.

DISAPPOINTMENT.

THE following day was occupied by the young man in superintending the arrangements of his friend's burial, and examining into his private affairs. What Mr. Brown's salary was he knew not; but it was certain that he had had no independent income of his own. By the terms of his letter it was apparent that he had designed to choose Williams as the only heir for whatever little property he might leave. As the will (if will it could be called) was informal, Williams had some scruples as to his right of claiming the effects of the deceased, and therefore thought it advisable to consult an *aroué* upon the subject. That worthy very soon eased his doubts by observing that as Mr. Brown had declared that he (Williams) was his only friend, and that he had no relations or connections living, it was as plain as possible that Williams was fully entitled to his goods, chattels, and so forth ; and strongly urged him to take possession of them at once, ere others might think fit to appropriate them in his room.

Mr. Brown had left in money three hundred francs, in notes, which were screwed up in an envelope and deposited, as he had said, in his desk. Also, a small money-box, heavy enough to be thoroughly pleasant, but which, when opened, was found to contain only coppers, it being a habit of the old man to put away his odd sous, not from any miserly emotion, but simply because he used to say to himself, " Some of these days I may want them ; and, changed into francs, they will at all events provide one with bread and butter in an emergency."

At a rough computation, his books, his odds and ends of furniture, his money, and one or two other things, Williams found to be worth about five hundred francs ; in round numbers, twenty pounds English. Such was the estate of a Man of Letters ! From this a fair sum was to be deducted for his funeral expenses, and for his rent, which was owing for the fortnight, and of which M. Mascot took care to remind Williams at the very first and earliest opportunity.

It was a dull day for poor Williams. With death within and uncertainty without, life was to him very full of gloom. He gazed out of the window, and saw the sun shining, and people walking below, talking and laughing, or whistling, or singing, and he thought how little that sun, or those people, cared for the silent heart that lay waiting to be enshrouded in its bed of earth, without an eye to deplore its stillness, without a heart to mourn its departure, but one; and he, the friend only of a few days!

There was a soberness in the fancy, in spite of its unreasonableness; and he felt that he could almost wish to be in the dead man's place, so calmly he lay, so peaceful amidst the thunders of the warring world around, so careless of the present, of the future; and of the past so mindless of each thought that might occur to embitter or to gladden his soul. Then he wondered that if *he* were dead what eye would shed a tear over him? There was Rosalie—but how long would Rosalie remember him? It was strange that this young man never thought either of his father or his mother. True, there was a yearning in his heart for something that it wanted; for something that it knew not, yet which it coveted. But a true friend—a wife—might have satisfied this craving. To him the words father, mother, were empty sounds. He had introduced them in his writings; he had heard them repeated in conversation; but then he had also written and heard the word "heaven;" yet not less vague were his notions of the one word than of the others. How could it be otherwise? How, even, but for education, should he have known the source, the origin of his being? Nature gave him the yearning—but she satisfied it not. She provided him with an enigmatical dream—but she lent him conjectures only to solve it.

The imagination of the young man might create in the dim past the phantoms of a love he was doomed not to know. A father, a mother, he might have evoked from the depths of fancy, and reared these airy shadows in his heart as things to wonder at and to adore. But the faith that prompts the human mind to worship those Invisibles in which it is instructed by others, was here wanting. He knew himself to be the creator of those phantoms with which he sought to supply the sacred cravings of his heart; and, mingled with the gladness of the love conceived by him, came the trembling and the doubt at the unreality of his own conceptions. The hunger of his love demanded something solid; it came not, and by degress he ceased to think or to conjecture. Sometimes he wondered; but the anxiety had passed. His heart still yearned, but the yearning had settled into a habit, and was no longer a pain.

It was with a beating heart that he arose next morning and entered his little sitting-room, to see if there were a letter to him from the London editor. But he was disappointed, and mechanically he performed his toilet, wondering whether any reply would come, and when. In spite of himself he discovered that he had made up his mind the answer would be favourable. This distressed him, for he well knew that should it be in the negative his disappointment would be keen, almost unbearable. Yet how impotent is the will to combat the emotions of the heart, the thoughts of the mind! Vainly he sought to subdue, to dissipate this secret conviction; it possessed him with unconquerable strength, and at last he was compelled to yield to it. "Perhaps," he thought, "the presentiment may prove correct." And his cheek flushed at the bare idea; but he cursed himself the next moment for his folly. "Poor

Mr. Brown thought he would live to finish his manuscript. There is *one* instance of the value of presentiments."

At twelve o'clock the coffin-bearers came to fetch away the last of the old man ; and at one the funeral was over. Sadly Williams returned home ; his thoughts full of the poor student, and his last act in leaving him his little all. His eyes were red as if with weeping. Well, he was an only friend—and he had buried him! The world seemed almost vacant to him now; he felt as if he were alone. And this is always the result of death in those we know. Men wither and fall away around us every day, every hour, yet we note not their departure—though they perish in thousands, we miss them not. *One* dies, and the world is suddenly desolate—the heavens are black —we are alone. And why ? because that *one* was a friend!

"*Il y a une lettre pour vous en haut, monsieur,*" said M. Mascot, who opened the door to him.

" From England ? "

" *Oui, monsieur.*"

In three bounds Williams had gained his apartment and stood looking at the letter. M. Mascot was quite right; the letter was from

England, and, moreover, the handwriting was the editor's, well-known by reason of his frequent communication with Mr. Brown.

It was a supreme moment for the young man; if favourable, it promised him a sufficient competence, a fair position, and present comfort. If unfavourable, want, hardship, perhaps starvation, unless he could devise some means of securing for himself an occupation.

He tore the envelope open with a trembling hand, and opening the enclosure, read as follows:

"—— Fleet Street, &c.

" SIR,

" In reply to your communication, I regret to have to inform you that your desire to be employed upon our staff as our Paris correspondent cannot be entertained. I thank you for your intimation of the death of Mr. Brown, whose loss I much regret, and am sorry to inform you that the receipt of your letter compelled the instant dispatch of another gentleman to supply his place.

" Yours obediently,

" SAMUEL SCROGGINS."

Here was a vindication of the truth of a

human presentiment! Oh, bitter mockery! that we should be buoyed high up by hope, only to render more headlong and crushing our later fall!

The letter fell from his hands, and he bowed his head upon his breast. The disappointment of the poor boy—he was but a boy after all!—was cruel. Yet he had had no right to expect anything else. In the arena of Literature such a blow as this was a flea-bite. He might have found comfort had he remembered that men had grown grey in labours which had been spurned—calumniated—crushed,—ay, and in the presence of the bleeding hearts of the aged, trembling, weeping toilers themselves! The ancient fable of the two fish cast upon the rock is good. Had the young man remembered the woe of others, his own disappointment might have lost more quickly something of its own intensity.

He remained for a long time in the position he had at first assumed, as if unable to raise his head and meet the light that entered through the windows. His mind was chaotic with the tumult of many passions. But rage predomi-nated; for this is the emotion that dogs the heel of every great disappointment. Rage at himself for cherishing the hope; rage at the distant stranger for denying it; rage at Fate for the position he now occupied; rage at the whole world from whom he had met with but such little kindness, and that, wrung out of it either by the helplessness of his childhood, the amiability of his disposition, or the zeal of his industry,—this was the passion that infused its poison in his heart—a heart yet young and plastic as the wax, to be moulded by every circumstance of shifting fate—and that caused him at last to leap from his chair, to smite his hand heavily upon the table, and to cry aloud with an oath, " I'll do it; it is my only hope—my only resource. If that fails me, then let me seek death!" The next moment he had descended the stairs, and had passed out into the street.

He walked along gazing earnestly into the shops as he passed, until he paused before a window in which were exposed a number of books for sale. Opening the door he walked in, and accosted a man who stood reading behind the counter.

" Do you purchase books here ?"

" Yes, sir. We prefer exchanging them, however."

"No—I don't mean exchange; do you give money, that's what I mean?"

The man looked angrily at this irritated young customer, and said,—

"Is monsieur certain that he knows what he means?"

"That's my affair!" retorted Williams; "you're an impertinent fellow—that's something else that I mean. Do you understand me?"

"*Nom d'un chien!*" muttered the man, "what do you mean by entering my shop to insult me? I'll call the police in in a moment, if you don't take yourself off."

Williams doubled his fist and glared at the man with dilated nostrils and clenched teeth. The man thought that he was going to attack him, and screwed up his mouth preparatory to shrieking "help." But even as he did so, Williams had turned his back upon him and had left the shop.

This incident furnished that bookseller with cause for a week's maledictions against "*le caractère brutal de messieurs les sacrés boule-dogues!*"

Williams continued his voyage down the street, inspecting the shops as he passed until he stopped before and entered the fellow of that he had so recently quitted. This time he was determined to subdue his bad-humour.

The same questions having been repeated and answered, Williams said, "I have some books at home which I am anxious to dispose of. It is not far. If you like to accompany me at once, the business can be settled, and you can take your purchase away with you."

"Oh, certainly," said the man, "I will go with you myself;" and leaving his shop in charge of an urchin, he proceeded with the young man to the Rue Vincennes.

"There they are," said Williams, pointing to some twenty-five or thirty volumes which had been the property of Mr. Brown, and which were ranged upon a side table against the wall. "Look at them, and name me what you think to be their value."

The bookseller did so, taking down one after the other, and closely inspecting them. "They're all very dry," said he, shaking his head : "they are not what I call customers' books.

"Perhaps not; but still they are worth something."

"The bindings are middling," said the man,

"and that's about the best part of them. Well, I will give monsieur eighteen francs!"

"Why, that's about twelve sous a piece!" exclaimed Williams, angrily.

"Well, twenty francs, monsieur."

"No: a sovereign: that's twenty-five francs, and you shall have them."

"Come," said the man, soothingly, who perceived that the books were worth three times the money, "we'll split the difference; shall I call it twenty-two francs, fifty centimes?"

"Let it be so, then. Give me the money, and take your books."

The man handed him the amount, and then tying up the volumes in several straps which he mysteriously produced out of various pockets, he slung them over his shoulder and departed, groaning beneath their weight, downstairs.

Williams went to a drawer and took out the notes which Brown had bequeathed him. These he spread upon the table, and taking out all the money he had in his pocket, he laid it by their side. I should have said that he had converted the copper contents of the money-box into silver: and found the whole to amount to five francs.

"Three hundred and twenty-two and a half," he said, counting, " and five, and six and a half; total three hundred and thirty-four francs. One hundred for the burial, eighteen for the rent, seven for myself,—that leaves me two hundred and nine francs. Very well ; now we shall see."

He placed the sum he had last mentioned in his pocket and redeposited the remainder in the drawer. Then he put his head out of the window, and consulted a clock which projected some distance down the street, over a jeweller's shop.

"It is a quarter to seven," he muttered; "I will wait an hour."

CHAPTER VI.

THE HOUSE IN THE RUE ANTOINE SARBOTIÈRE.

I HAVE before spoken of a little door painted brown, belonging to a house situated in the Rue Antoine Sarbotière. I will now raise the latch, and, with the reader's permission, venture to conduct him in. But, first of all, a word for the locality.

It was eight o'clock in the evening, and the night outside was dark; so dark indeed as to render the Rue Antoine Sarbotière, which was one of the worst lighted streets in Paris, dismal and almost forbidding. A thoroughfare, sufficiently brilliant with lamps and shops, traversed it at its foot, thereby making it by the contrast more uninviting and unpleasant.

In the daytime, when the light came down from without, the shutters of all but one of the houses—and all the houses were private—were thrown open; and though the darkened blinds pretty well served to make gloomy the interior of the rooms, there was yet a certain openness about them which, when contrasted with the single house and its closed shutters, seemed almost innocent. What all these houses were, by whom they were maintained, and whether the voice of rumour or tradition be true, I have had neither the curiosity nor the time to discover. My business is only with one of them, and that the most ominous of all, for neither light by night is emitted from it, nor light by day suffered to enter it.

On opening the door, however, you would have been surprised at two things: first, that the door itself appeared to be kept constantly open; and, secondly, that the moment you entered you discovered yourself to be enveloped in a flood of light, imparted by two powerful bull's-eye lamps suspended from the ceiling.

At the end of this passage stood a green baize door, studded with brass nails, and which you opened by pulling *towards* you. As you did so, the confused murmur of voices within would strike your ear, and you would observe that another door, also of green baize, and studded with brass nails, had to be pushed *before* you, ere you could enter the apartment beyond.

It was astonishing how these two doors deadened the sound of the voice; for when they were opened, the noise within was as great as the silence without had been profound. But then this might have been owing to the unexpected transition from peace to confusion.

On this particular night, and at the hour of eight, this is the scene that would have greeted your eye upon entering this room.

In the centre of the apartment, and illumined by a chandelier, stood an oblong table, covered with square patches, each being labelled with figures, and marked at its side by a name. At the head of this board, not unlike in shape to, and of about the same dimensions as, an ordinary billiard-table, was seated an elderly man, who, with a solemn countenance, occasionally turned a species of fixed teetotum with a ball in it, the rattling of which, as it was revolved with amazing rapidity, seemed to be the signal for a crowd of persons who surrounded the table to lean forward with an eager curiosity, and to hold their breath until the rattling noise had ceased. Each side of the table, and also the foot, was occupied by a man who held in his hand a little ivory rake, which he employed, when the teetotum had ceased spinning, to collect into a heap before him the coins or the paper that were plentifully sprinkled about the patches on the board.

If my reader has ever visited Homburg, and traversed the apartments of that Hall dedicated to the worst passions of man, and called the Kursäal, he will recognise in this the miniature representation of the *roulette* table. Indeed, the proprietor of this little house in the Rue Antoine Sarbotière seemed to have carried his imitation to an unnecessary state of perfection : since he employed three *croupiers* besides himself to preside at a table where one would have been ample; and to employ three rakes when the fingers of one hand would have been more than sufficient.

That he had been fortunate enough to secure a very fair " connection," was evident in the numbers that, even at that early hour, already thronged his room, and who by their manner seemed to denote themselves *habitués*, or frequenters long accustomed to the scene.

They were as motley a crew, taking them all in all, as ever the eye rested upon—numbering together about thirty-five persons, and these of all nations, rank, manners, and appearance. The predominating element was French, as was ren-

dered apparent by the loudness of their conversation, the vehemence of their gesticulation, and
the frequency of their facial contortions. There
were also one or two Englishmen amongst the
crowd near the table, and these had been, or
were, evidently playing high—for those behind
sometimes nodded in their direction, and spoke
together in whispers, and not a few squeezed
their way through to get near and inspect them
and their game for themselves.

At one end of the apartment there stood
another door, covered with green baize, leading
to another room.

"Make your game, gentlemen," cried the proprietor from the end of the table; "make your
game!"

Several hands were protruded from the crowd,
and shortly after, some napoleons and silver of
all value were sparkling upon the table. In the
middle there was placed a bank note.

"Whose paper is that?" asked a Frenchman
standing by the side of one of the Englishmen.

"Mine," answered the Briton, turning sharply
round, and scrutinising the inquirer's face with
a look of contempt.

"Monsieur is daring. Is monsieur a winner?"

"Sixteen hundred francs."

"You play with extraordinary luck!"

The Englishman shrugged his shoulders.

"Never mind what luck it is, provided it *is* luck."

"*Sans doute!* Ah, the game begins."

"Have you staked anything?"

"I never play," said the Frenchman.

"Then what's your motive in coming here?"

"To study human nature."

"There's no pull in that? Come, risk a florin on the next turn."

"Not for twenty millions of florins."

The Englishman turned his back upon his companion with an exclamation of contempt. At the same moment, a voice cried,—

"Ah, M. Villiers, how are you?"

The Frenchman raised his head, and murmured, "Ah, it is the hunchback Sloman." Then, nodding to him, he said,—

"You here again?"

"Yes," answered Sloman, paddling his deformed body through the crowd with his elbows; "here I am, with five napoleons in my pocket for luck—five's a lucky number, you know."

"Well, you're too late for this round," answered M. Villiers, inspecting Sloman's face with admiration—the admiration, I mean, that a connoisseur bestows on the impossible countenance of a Hogarth, or the grotesque attitude of a Cruikshank.

"Are you going to win or lose?"

Sloman snapped his thigh with vehemence as he answered,—

"Win, of course."

"What will content you?"

"Well, I have brought a fiver; if I make twenty out of it, I shall consider it a good night's work."

"*Tiens, c'est le bossu!*" said a voice behind him.

Sloman turned, and bowing to the speaker with mock solemnity, answered,—

"*Oui, c'est le bossu.* What do you want with him?"

"I have come to see you play," said the man accosted.

"Well, you shall be gratified in a minute. I——"

He stopped suddenly, and uttered an exclamation of surprise; then, uprearing himself on his toes, commenced vigorously nodding to somebody at the end of the room ; at the same time he plucked M. Villiers by the coat-tail.

"What is it ? " asked M. Villiers.

"Don't you see him ? " said Sloman, nodding in the direction of the door.

M. Villiers looked, and exclaimed,—

"Why, it's your friend of the Café Victoire ! What does he do here ? "

"I'll go and see."

And once more Sloman paddled himself through the crowd, and made towards the door.

"And so you have come to inspect our proceedings, Mr. Williams, have you ? " he said, laughing grotesquely. " Ha, ha ! welcome to this vale — this vale of — I was going to say tears, but I won't; for look at the faces around you — ain't they jolly-looking ? " and Sloman swept the room with his arms.

" Are you not Mr. Sloman ? " asked Williams, who was pale, and apparently agitated in his manner.

" That's my name ; we've both got good memories, eh? "

" This is my first visit here," said Williams ; " and if I am successful it will be my last."

" Ay, you must break the bank to-night, Mr.

Williams. Let's draw near the table, and see what's going on."

And pioneering the way for Williams, he conducted him almost to the side of M. Villiers.

"I am sorry to see you here, sir," said the Frenchman, in a low voice; "especially in that man's society. Did I not caution you?"

"Thank you," answered Williams, haughtily. "Your advice is doubtless well meant; but let me assure you it is not required."

M. Villiers shrugged his shoulders.

"Please yourself; but, as the elder of the two. I thought I was only doing my duty by offering you a caution."

And edging away, he withdrew himself from the young man's presence.

But Williams had not heard the remark. His eyes had been fixed on the table before him, and he awaited with breathless interest the result of the stoppage of the teetotum at the head. He was too absorbed even to notice the terrible eagerness expressed in the many odd-looking faces that were bending, some white, some yellow, some red, towards the table.

At last the proprietor shouted out something; in a moment the men by the sides of the table had raked up the money that was scattered about upon it; and a man near Williams stretched forth his hand and received some money from a croupier. Williams turned to look at him. The man's face was radiant with smiles, and he extended between his thumb and forefinger a little *rouleau* of gold.

"I put down five napoleons; I win this," he said to a companion near him.

"Thou art lucky. 'Tis multiplying five by five."

"*Corpo di Bacco!* this is the way to grow rich."

"Or poor," said his companion.

"I think I shall try my luck," exclaimed Williams, the expression of his face plainly showing how he sympathised with the general excitement.

"Wait!" said the hunchback, who stood beside him; "see me play first. If I am lucky, pursue my choice of numbers; if unlucky, do the other thing. You mustn't be a loser here for the first night. Besides, you don't know the game, and should watch it a little; perhaps somebody's luck may give you a hint."

He had dropped his rude, intrusive manner of speaking, and his voice was more subdued, as if to conciliate Williams, whom he perceived occasionally glanced at him with a distrustful look.

"Make your game, gentlemen!" cried the proprietor, from the head of the table.

Sloman took a napoleon out of his pocket, and placed it upon a square labelled with the figure seven.

"Seven," said he, "is a lucky figure. It is the sacred number throughout the East; and you'll find it considered so by most people."

" *V 'la là une sottise!*" said a voice near him; "just as if seven were better than eight, or eight than nine."

"Well," retorted Sloman, angrily, "and if I choose to consider it lucky, what's that to you?"

"Hunchbacks are always superstitious," remarked the man, in German, to a thick-moustachioed friend; "don't you remember Father Schorchells?"

"Ha! ha! So, eh?" said the moustachioed friend, hoisting up his shoulders and mimicking the deformity of a hump.

Sloman grew scarlet with rage. "Isn't it a curse," he muttered to Williams, "that the use of the poignard or the stiletto is forbidden in this country? What would I give for permission to make a hole in some of these impudent thieves, just to let out a little of their sauce and impertinence!"

At this moment the rattling of the ball near the croupier indicated that the game had commenced. Sloman bent forward with suspended breath, forming one only of the crowd of motley faces, whose gaze, riveted on the revolving destiny, expressed every emotion, from stolid indifference to the most torturing expectation.

The ball stopped; there was a sound of money being swept away; a few hands were stretched out; and the dead silence that had preceded the event was dissipated by a general tumult of voices, some speaking angrily, some uttering the coarsest maledictions, a few laughing. Williams looked at Sloman. "Are you a winner?" he asked.

He gave his shoulders a fierce shrug as he answered "No."

"Are you going to try again?"

"Of course I shall!"

"My friend, you perceive I was right in ridiculing your holy number!" said a voice behind.

"*Allez au diable!*" muttered Sloman, without turning his head.

The voice laughed, "Was'nt that said exactly like Father Schorchells?"

"Yes," answered the thick-mustachioed friend. "Look! this is how Father Schorchells would have answered," and again he mimicked the aspect of a hunchback.

Father Schorchells, as embodied by Sloman, seemed to afford these two men much merriment, for they laughed loud and long.

"Hang you and Father Schorchells, too; go, and leave me alone," and the hunchback glared at them with a flashing eye.

"Come, are you going to stake again?" asked Williams.

"Don't let us stop here!" exclaimed the enraged hunchback. "Come into the *rouge et noir* room."

"Where is that?"

"Through that green door at the end there. It is not only quieter, but the chances are more equal. The other night I made nearly three hundred francs, by constantly backing the red."

"Very well, lead the way; we can always return here;" and he followed Sloman in the direction of the door that he had indicated.

The room devoted to the game of *rouge et noir* was much of the same size as that in which the *roulette* was placed. Sofas were arranged around it, and in the centre was placed a table, at which sat a man, shuffling a pack of cards. A few persons were congregated near him, at whom he occasionally looked up, soliciting them for stakes.

"You begin, Mr. Williams, this time," said Sloman. "Perhaps, if you are lucky, you will bring me luck. Take my advice, and try the red."

"Very well." Then addressing the croupier, he said, "*Rouge*." When the stakes were collected, the man flung a card down. It was black.

"Never mind," said Sloman; "try again: but stick to the red."

Williams was evidently in a state of great agitation; his face was pale, and his hands violently trembled. Sloman noticed his emotion, and whispered,—

"You'll soon get used to it. I was nervous the first night; but you see I've quite got over it."

"What is it, gentlemen?" said the croupier.

"*Rouge*," answered Williams.

The card turned up again: this time it was red.

"Bravo!" exclaimed Sloman; "I'll wager a thousand pounds to a franc that you have a run of luck to-night. Mind and stick to the red!"

Again Williams played, and again won. He was now a winner of fifteen francs. His face was flushed with excitement, and he regarded Sloman with a smile.

"You're quite right," he exclaimed, in an excited whisper; "red is the lucky colour."

For five successive times the young man backed the red, and each time he was a winner. His luck was now beginning to attract attention, and every eye followed his movements.

"Now let me have a fling," said Sloman, ecstatically. "I'll pursue the luck that I have pointed out to you; and you'll see me break the bank."

"What is it, gentlemen?" asked the croupier.

"Red," said Sloman.

A card was flung down, and black turned up.

"There goes my second napoleon," said the hunchback, angrily. "I have only three left!"

He staked again, and again lost.

"Try the black," whispered Williams.

He placed a napoleon on the black; the card turned up red. A coarse oath escaped the hunchback's lips, and his face grew flushed with anger.

"You've brought me ill-luck," he muttered,

turning a sour eye upon Williams. "I have never lost successively like this before."

But Williams was too delighted to be angry. In a few moments he had made fifty francs—and this, thanks to the hunchback.

"Nonsense!" he exclaimed. "Toss a two-sous bit, and let heads mean black, and tails red."

Sloman threw the coin in the air, and caught it in his hand.

"What is it?" asked Williams.

"Tails!"

"Then back the red."

"What shall it be, gentlemen?" asked the croupier.

"A napoleon on the red," answered the hunch-back.

"*Bon.*" The croupier shuffled the cards, and threw one out. It was black.

The hunchback literally foamed with rage. The expression of his face was so grotesque as to provoke laughter from some one on the other side of the table. Sloman shook his fist at the man, and cried,—

"What are you laughing at?"

Whereupon everybody grew suddenly convulsed

with laughter, and Sloman, his face dark with anger, turned to Williams.

"Wherever I go, I am persecuted by these wretches!" he shrieked, rather than spoke. "Not content with seeing me lose my money, they insult my shape."

"You should keep calm," answered Williams, whose head, half turned at first by his good fortune, was slowly recovering its equilibrium. "They laugh at your anger, not at your person."

"How would you have me keep calm after losing a hundred francs? Add this to a hundred and fifty, and that will make a loss of two hundred and fifty francs in two nights."

"Try once more. Your stakes are too high; content yourself with half a napoleon."

"I only brought out five with me; and I've lost them all," said Sloman, gloomily.

"Well, here's ten francs I can lend you. Try your luck with this," and he placed the money in his hand.

Sloman approached the table, and after a moment's consideration, backed the red. He lost.

With another malediction, he stamped his foot heavily upon the ground, and folding his arms on his breast, stood savagely silent.

"I shall try again," said Williams; "perhaps your ill-luck will prove my fortune."

The spectators knew that he had been fortunate; and as he drew near they made way for him. He backed the red and won; again, again, and again he proved successful.

"*Voilà une affaire!*" cried some voices. Even the croupier raised his head, and inspected him with curiosity.

As he was about renewing the game, his arm was suddenly seized, and a voice whispered in his ear,—

"Young man, do not be rash. You have had luck: do not tempt Fortune."

He turned and encountered the supplicating face of M. Villiers.

The young man ran his eye over him, and angrily exclaimed,—

"Your advice is not only unseasonable, but impertinent! If it is repeated I shall accept it as an insult, and act accordingly."

The Frenchman glanced at him for a moment with a look of mournful surprise; then muttering, "You shall be troubled by me no more, sir," he turned his back upon him and left the apartment.

" What was M. Villiers talking to you about ? " asked Sloman, approaching him.

" He is an impertinent old fellow," answered Williams; " like all old men, he fancies he has a right to advise. I do not think, however, he will bore me again."

" You are right; he is impertinent, and I am charmed to find you so ready to reject his impudent advice: for it is impudent, as it isn't wanted. I suppose he told you to leave off playing ? "

" He did."

" Bah! that's *his* game! Never mind; if I were you, I'd follow the lucky tide that seems to have set in for you. I've become pretty experienced in this, and predict for you a speedy fortune. What now, may I ask, are your winnings ? "

" Five hundred francs."

" Commence again, and don't leave off until you have doubled it."

Williams needed not this incitement. His mind had become penetrated with the new passion that had been so suddenly developed. The magic chalice of success had been placed at his lips; he had drunken deep of the subtle liquid, and his blood was in a ferment with the intoxicating draught.

The croupier looked up to him with an inquiring glance.

"Is it red again, monsieur?"

"No; two napoleons on the black."

A murmur of excitement rose amongst the the crowd, and a number of eager faces leant forward to view the result.

A card was thrown down, and the croupier cried, "*Noir.*"

This luck was incredible. The group around the table eyed the young Englishman with an almost superstitious gravity. Sloman was at his side caressing him on the back.

"I can forget my own ill-luck in your good-luck," he whispered. "This is delicious. Go in for the thousand, and when you've touched it, leave off."

With such success as his, the thousand francs were soon gained. Then Sloman put his arm through the young man's, and drew him gently from the table.

"You have hitherto adopted my advice," he said; "now don't think me rude by my urging you still to adhere to it. Evidently I am sent to help you on to an easy and rapid fortune ; so, in the character of a good angel, let me beg of you to play no more to-night. You have made a thousand francs—in English, forty pounds—and you had better rest upon your oars for awhile. If luck should turn, you'd never forgive yourself for continuing the risk."

The allusion to "the good angel" made Williams laugh loudly. There was a certain solid sense, however, in Sloman's advice, which Williams perceived, and which he came to the conclusion it was advisable to adopt. Evidently, he thought, this fellow understands the thing better than I do; and as his advice has been so far true, I think I cannot do better than to abide by what he says.

The cool of the street soon tempered the imagination of the young man, heated by the glare, the excitement and the confusion of the "hell" he had deserted. But he had little time for reflection, as Sloman was at his side talking with the rapidity and vehemence that made his grotesque appearance even more remarkable.

"Look! we had no refreshments during our hard labour—nothing to atone for the constant strain upon the attention. So I tell you what

I propose doing: come home with me to my apartments; you will there find grog and cigars, and—" he added, bowing with ridiculous solemnity—"a welcome from your obedient servant."

Williams thanked him, but said it was late.

"Well, and what has the hour to do with it? A man don't make a thousand francs every night! Besides, you owe it to me in a measure: so come home, and let's drink success to each other!"

Williams remembered that there was no especial reason *why* he should be home early: for there was nobody to sit up for him, and nobody to expect him. And moreover, was he not his own master now? Had Mr. Brown been living he might perhaps have evinced some anxiety to maintain either a just or seeming character for regularity. But he was now alone: himself only his own master and judge. And as yet he had not learned to fear himself.

"As you say," he replied, "this is a night I ought to render memorable some way or other. A thousand francs is forty pounds; and forty pounds, as I have gained it, is worth forty hundred, when compared with the labours of others to acquire the same money. So I'll accept your invitation, and drink a glass of spirits with you at your house."

"Bravo!" said Sloman, "that's right. We shall be good friends yet, I see. Never mind my face. The heart's the thing whereby to test the conscience of a king! That's not Shakspeare —that's sense! Ha! ha! ha! come along—this way!" And passing his arm through Williams' they turned the corner of the Rue Antoine Sarbotière and walked away.

CHAPTER VII.

As they entered the Rue Colville, Sloman pointed to a house and exclaimed, "I wish I was worth the wealth of the old cove who lives there."

"Do you mean who lives at No. 13?"

Sloman nodded.

"I am acquainted with the inmates of that house."

"Indeed," said Sloman, looking up into his companion's face.

"Yes—both old Gautier and his daughter."

"A pretty girl—that daughter of his."

"Yes — very pretty," answered Williams, drily.

"I am perfectly in love with her from watching her from my window," said Sloman. "Couldn't you put me in the way of making friends with her?"

Williams seized him suddenly by the arm, so threateningly, that the hunchback uttered an exclamation of pain, and cried, "Let go! what do you mean?"

"I mean," said Williams, relaxing his grasp, "that I love Mam'selle Gautier. Do you understand? Think what you like: but don't open your lips in my presence about her unless it is to speak well of her."

The hunchback shrugged his shoulders. "I understand you," he said. "All right. Don't fear. I shan't prove a rival. This way."

And extracting a latch-key from his pocket, he applied it to the door of the house he occupied, and ushered his friend upstairs.

There was not much difference between his apartments and those of Williams' in the Rue Vincennes. Sloman's perhaps were a little better furnished, having a clock on the mantlepiece, two shepherdesses and two jars: articles which it had not probably entered M. Mascot's head to provide.

"It is eleven o'clock!" exclaimed Williams, consulting this little clock. "How rapidly the time has passed to be sure!"

"You have been three hours making a thousand

francs. That's at the rate of thirteen pounds, some odd shillings an hour! Well, you have no reason to complain," said Sloman, pushing a chair to his guest and ringing the bell.

Presently a sleepy woman entered the room and demanded to know his wants.

" Provide us with hot water and glasses," answered Sloman; "and then you may go to bed."

When this was done the two gentlemen seated themselves in easy chairs, and proceeded to brew themselves some spirits and water. The excite-ment under which Williams had been labouring during the evening had not yet passed away. This unexpected acquisition of a thousand francs to his means had provoked in his heart feelings too intense to be easily subdued. Indeed, he could not credit his good luck. It seemed as if he had suddenly fallen upon a mine of gold of which the supply was inexhaustible, and which promised him a future as bright, as glorious, as fair, as it had been before bleak and barren. As he sat in his chair eyeing Sloman, he fancied the whole to be a dream, from which he was soon to wake to a certainty of destitution made keener by the brightness of the present vision. So powerfully did this fancy control him, that his hand mechanically sought his pocket wherein he had deposited the money, so that by the touch he might prove real what he imagined to be an hallucination.

Sloman noticed the action. "That is right," he exclaimed, "take it out and count it. You say you have won a thousand francs, but I believe you must have won more."

Williams silently extracted the money from his pocket, and laid it upon the table. His winnings had been paid him chiefly in gold, but there were also one or two notes and a fair sprinkling of silver amidst the yellow heap. He proceeded leisurely to count it, Sloman the while regarding the coins with an avaricious stare.

"Well, what do you make it?"

"A thousand and fifteen francs."

"Ha! I wish to heaven I had had your luck to-night! When I first started at this game I thought to make a rapid fortune; and so I did at the commencement, for in three nights I had won nearly eighteen hundred francs. But after that I lost it all again, and with something more besides."

"It's all a matter of see-saw, I suppose; you

must expect sometimes to be down, as well as up."

"Of course. My misfortune is not my ill-luck, but my deformity. I am constantly insulted by the scurvy crew that hang about the rooms. You heard them to-night, did you not?" asked Sloman, his eyes alive with the lurid glow of rage.

"Bah! what are they to you?"

"True, I'm a fool to mind it. Are you drinking?"

"Yes, thank you."

Sloman poured himself out a brimming bumper, which he held up before Williams. "Here's my toast," he said. "May you always have the luck you have had to-night; may you soon win a large fortune; may I at once begin to have an equal success; and may we both soon make rapid fortunes!" With which Christian-like conclusion, he gulped down half the contents of the glass, and wiped his eyes with a red silk pocket-handkerchief.

"How did you first of all find out that gambling-house?" asked Williams.

"I can't tell you exactly—unless it was instinct," said Sloman, with a grin.

" How do you mean instinct ? "

" I only say instinct to supply what I cannot explain. The truth is, I was in a café one night, and I heard the name of the house, and the street mentioned, though by whom I didn't know, for I never thought of turning my head to look. Well, the next night I found myself in the house they had mentioned."

" And a loser ? "

" No, a winner."

" Ah, I remember, a loser afterwards."

" Yes, of two thousand one hundred francs."

As he spoke Williams looked at him hard, and then around the room. In truth he was rather puzzled by the man before him. Here was one who was living in a by no means fashionable quarter of the town, in a little street, and occupying apartments on the third floor of the most common-place of houses, talking bigly of his thousands of francs, his losses and his gains. Either the man was a boaster, or else he was most studious of avoiding by external pomp all appearance of wealth.

" How long do you propose remaining in Paris ? " asked Williams, anxious to start a topic

that might lead the hunchback into some dis-
closures concerning himself.

Sloman misunderstood the motive of this
question, and answered with a smile, "Oh, a
long time yet."

"But of course you will soon be giving up the
gambling house?"

"Why should I?"

"At the rate you are going on in your losses
your means must compel you to visit it no more—
unless you are a millionaire?"

"No, I'm not a millionaire. But how do you
mean my losses? I may recover every sixpence
of them to-morrow night."

"True; but supposing you should not."

"Hang it!" replied Sloman, rather angrily,
"what's the use of supposing a thing that hasn't
yet occurred? You don't want to ruin me before
I *am* ruined, do you?" he added, resuming his
grin.

"Certainly not. However, *I* shall go there no
more."

Sloman raised his hands and uttered an exclamation of astonishment. "What! *you* won't
go there any more? You're joking!"

"No; I am quite serious."

"Then you'll be cruelly wronging yourself—that's all I've got to say," said Sloman, turning his side to Williams, and knocking the ashes of his pipe out on the table. "But," he continued, suddenly, "you're joking!"

"Look! I have won a thousand francs. I have met with an extraordinary success. Had I remained in the house, I might, perhaps, have pursued it. But now that I am out of it, I shall return no more."

Sloman grasped a brandy-bottle, and poured some of its contents into Williams's glass; then mixing it with a little water, he held it to his companion's lips. "Drink," he cried, "and drown that absurd thought in this. Drown it at once, before it gets a firm hold of you, and by frightening you into primness, ruins you!"

Williams laughed, but refused the proffered tumbler. Sloman fell back into his seat, waving his head with a deprecating gesture. "'There is a tide,'" he exclaimed, "'in the affairs of men, that, taken at the flood, leads on to fortune.' That's one of the most hackneyed sayings in the language, which plainly shows how true it is. Now you have that tide, and it is at its flood; and if you don't avail yourself of it, never blame yourself if you should die in a workhouse."

"But how do you know that I am not a man of means: independent of all such resources as the *roulette* or the *rouge-et-noir* table can supply?"

"If you are," said the hunchback, shrugging his shoulders, "so much the better for you."

"Well, I am not. Frankly, I am very poor; and that was my motive for visiting that rendez-vous of gamblers."

"I suspected as much. I saw you were poor by your dress."

"And how do you stand in the books of Fortune?" asked Williams, taking advantage of the hunchback's familiar manner to put the question to him.

"Now, what do you think I'm worth?" said Sloman, grinning.

"By your conversation, I should imagine you to be wealthy; by your habitation——"

"Poor?"

"No; but hardly rich."

The hunchback rose and went to a drawer, from which he extracted an account book. "Now you shall know exactly my position: my money

to a penny: here it all is." And, seating himself, he proceeded to refer to the pages of the
book in his hands.

"Some days ago," said he, "I left London
with thirteen hundred pounds in my pocket.
That was a pretty round sum, was it not?"

"Was that your whole capital?"

"Yes."

Williams remained silent, and Sloman said,
"So you see I am *not* a millionaire! Well, two
nights after my arrival, I won two, the night
after, three, the night after that, nine and five—as
I told you, about eighteen hundred francs. Then
I lost the whole of it, and four hundred francs
more. Then," continued he, following some
figures in the book with his finger, "I lost one,
two, three, four, five—but I detest reading 'em!
let this be the result: of thirteen hundred pounds,
I have eight hundred left—there!" and in a
sudden fit of anger he slammed the book down
upon the table.

"Five hundred pounds in nine days! that is
useful for me to recollect."

"Why?"

"Because it shows me my ultimate fate."

"If I didn't *know* you to have pluck, I should

fancy, from what you now say, that you are a bit of a coward. How long do you think a thousand francs will last you?"

Williams shrugged his shoulders. "Not long, I am afraid."

"Of course not. You'll soon be wanting more: and where are you to get it from?"

"I must work for it."

"Work, when it is to be coined by an amusement! Sweat and toil at a heart-breaking occupation for a few shillings a day in preference to a couple of hours' delicious excitement amidst heaps of wealth, a lump of which may perhaps be yours! No, no! you are a wise man—you don't want me to say more."

Williams rose from his seat, his face a little flushed with the effects of his drinking, and his manner agitated and nervous.

"Where are you going to?"

"Home."

"Why, man, it isn't twelve yet!"

"I am sleepy."

"I can give you a bed upstairs, if you like?"

"Thanks, the Rue de Vincennes is not very far off."

"Do you live in the Rue de Vincennes? why,

it is a walk from here of nearly three quarters of an hour."

"I know."

"Why don't you shift your lodgings? you are out of the world in the Rue de Vincennes. Come more this way—the world of Paris is around you here."

"I shall certainly be shifting soon, as I don't like my present position much."

"Of course; who could? I know the Rue de Vincennes well. You have a heap of dirty alleys and courts leading out of it; and on my soul, it is not fit for a gentleman. No, come down here —look, why didn't you take rooms in this house? I am the only lodger, and there are some capital apartments to let downstairs as well as up. You will be awfully comfortable: I'll guarantee that— and, moreover, you'll be conferring a boon on " —with his grotesque bow—"me, who pine for con- genial company—and have found it in you!"

Williams hesitated; the emotions of the even- ing had been too frequent and plentiful to permit him to reflect with precision or clearness. "I will think over it," he said.

"Do," answered the hunchback; "and if I can't find eloquence enough to induce you, let me see if that won't assist me!" He went to the window and drew up the blind; then beckoning to Williams to approach him, he pointed with his . finger to the house opposite, looking up at the same time into the young man's face with a wild, grotesque, singular smile. "You know who lives *there*, don't you?" he whispered.

Williams fixed his eyes with a fond look upon the house, and answered, "Yes."

"Isn't she enough to attract you to this neighbourhood?" continued the hunchback; "you have told me you love her: I believe you, and *that*, I say, ought to make you desert the Rue de Vincennes.—Ah!" he exclaimed, "look!" A light had been suddenly thrown from within on to one of the blinds on the second story: and against it was clearly marked the outline of a woman's form, standing for a few moments motionless. The hunchback still pointed, and the young lover bent forward, gazing with a throbbing heart on the shadow, which he well knew to be Rosalie's.

Suddenly the shadow disappeared, but the light was still left burning. "She is about retiring to rest," said Sloman; "ah, you should come here, man,—you should come here. See the advantage—besides, you are close to the Rue Antoine Sarbotière."

Williams looked at him in silence. The vision that had been so suddenly presented to him of Rosalie had aroused in his heart emotions of a wild and thrilling nature. He loved her: his tongue not alone had confessed it; but it was written on his heart. Yet what would avail his love without fortune? he could not wed her to poverty! In his present position he had not even a shelter to offer her—unless the Rue Antoine Sarbotière should supply him with means to take her to his heart. This was the thought that had caused him to turn and inspect the features of Sloman in silence.

"Well, what say you to my proposition? Speak the word and I will secure you at once any of the rooms you may like to choose."

"I will think over it."

"Do. Shall I see you to-morrow night?"

"Perhaps. If I make up my mind to come here I will drop you a line."

"Thanks." Then seizing his arm, Sloman said, in a mysterious whisper, "But apart from the advantages offered to you by being near *her*," and he nodded in the direction of the window as he spoke, "you must remember that our alliance has proved so far very fortunate to you, though not so to me. I told you to back the red, and my advice has given you a thousand francs. Now what may it profit you in the future? Don't laugh at my superstition! I am a bit of a believer in mysterious things of this kind; and am firmly convinced that where fortune will desert one, she will often assist two together. At all events such has proved the case to-night; and pray how are you to tell that it will not always prove so, until there is no longer any occasion to test it?"

Enthusiasm is always catching; and when a man argues with the appearance of being profoundly convinced of the truth of what he says, he will not often fail to impart something of his conviction to his hearer.

Williams listened to him in silence, and smiled when he had concluded; but his smile was not one of ridicule.

"Well," said he, "if our alliance can lead us both to fortune, by all means let us unite ourselves. But unlike you, I am not in the least superstitious. I am a believer in chance, or luck, but that is about all."

The hunchback solemnly shook his head.

> "There are more things in heaven and earth, Horatio,
> Than are dreamed of in your philosophy,"

he exclaimed.

"I must congratulate you upon your intimate knowledge of Shakspeare," said Williams, slightly laughing; "this is the third time you have quoted him to-night."

"Wouldn't I make a splendid Richard III. ?" exclaimed Sloman.

"Splendid," answered Williams, who really thought he would.

"If the gambling-house clears me out, I shall try the stage. When you have taken up your abode here I will amuse you by giving you some specimens of my stage powers."

"Thanks; and now farewell."

"Farewell. Mind and drop me a line."

"I will;" and shaking hands with the hunch-back, Williams went away.

The young man did not know enough of Sloman's character to suspect him of any design in his proposition. He perceived only in the hunchback a very singular specimen of the human kind, a heterogeneous mixture of passion, vice, merriment, and folly. Their marked development he attributed rather to the curvature of his spine than to the deformity of his mind; and whilst he contemplated with secret laughter so anomalous a creation, he experienced no fear lest his companionship should seduce him into a conduct worse than that which he had now self-willingly assumed. Moreover, whether fortuitously or not, he could not forget that Sloman was just in recalling to him the fact that to his suggestion, or advice, he had terminated his evening by finding himself to be the winner of a thousand francs.

Now a thousand francs to a young man in want, when thrown into the scale opposing the vices and ill-fame of a companion, has a marked effect in reducing the weight of his sins and equalizing the asperities of his character. The antecedents of Sloman—his past conduct—his present mode of life, were in reality nothing whatever to Williams. The hunchback had been accidentally the medium of placing in his way a means whereby affluence might perhaps be secured, and in a manner the most easy, the most delightful, and the most speedy. Whether a continued intercourse might profit him, remained yet to be discovered; but certain it was, that if his evening companionship were to be always so remunerative as it had proved, it was by all means sedulously to be cultivated, and this with a stolid indifference as to his character, his name, or anything else connected with him.

There was yet an obstruction, however, to his adoption of the hunchback's scheme which needed some consideration ere it could be surmounted. He well knew that Rosalie must have remarked the strange figure of the hunchback passing to and from his house, and he fancied that she might, perhaps, have taken a dislike, or a disgust, to the man which might extend itself to the lover when she should discover him to be his companion. But then this was only supposititious; he had no reason to suppose that Rosalie felt any dislike towards Sloman—indeed, that she had ever seen or noticed him: and even allowing this to be the case, there was no reason that Rosalie should know that Williams was his friend: for what was more natural than for the young lover to take up his abode near the residence of his *amorosa*, and in doing so find himself brought in contact with a man whom (for aught she might know) he had never before seen?

Such were the thoughts that chased the mind

of the young man as he walked home to his lodgings, and which resulted in a determination to fix upon the Rue Colville as his future residence. To be near Rosalie was a delight which only such a course could gratify: and as to Mr. Sloman, nothing was easier than to cut his acquaintance if he should not prove exactly the right thing. So on his arrival he addressed a few lines to Sloman, intimating to him his intention; and then tumbling into bed, lay awake the whole night thinking of Sloman, of Rosalie, of his future, and of the house in the Rue Antoine Sarbotière.

CHAPTER VIII.

INFLUENCE.

Two days passed away, and No. 22, Rue Colville owned, in addition to its hunchback, another lodger.

Sloman had paid one visit to the gambling-house, but had not met Williams. He had received his note, however, and was aware that he would be with him the next day. The young man did not arrive till after dark; he knew not why, but he felt that the step he was taking was not in unison with his own feelings; and perhaps this suspicion made him choose the dusk of the evening in which to perform his transit; Rosalie might see him, and this he was anxious to avoid. But why? Rosalie must sooner or later have seen him, and why not then?

Wrong always makes itself apparent in an undefinable dread of something. By this dread we are enabled to define between good and evil. But sometimes conscience whispers when the meditated step seems free from all taint of guilt. This was the case with Williams.

Sloman was at home when he entered, and met him with a welcome.

"It is truly jolly for me to have you in the house," he said; "we can smoke and drink and talk away to our hearts' content, and neither of us can feel dull. Now if we were separated, it would be the reverse."

Williams had taken the apartments situated on the floor above the hunchback's. They were cheaper, and he preferred them—he had said to Sloman, from an economical point of view—infinitely to the others.

But Sloman had laughed and exclaimed— "What nonsense! in a short time you will be returning to England, and taking a house in the most fashionable part of London."

At a quarter to nine the hunchback knocked at the door of Williams's room, and said,—

"I am off to the Rue Antoine Sarbotière; are you coming?"

"No; not to-night."

"Come along. Perhaps you may make a few hundreds."

"No; I shan't venture out to-night. You go and make them for me."

The hunchback laughed, and went down-stairs.

When he had knocked, Williams was seated in his chair, reposing his feet upon the fender, and reading a book. When he had gone, he laid the book down and commenced to think. After remaining lost in a reverie for some ten minutes, he rose, and going to the window, looked out. His eyes were fixed upon the windows opposite, upon which he had seen, a few nights before, reflected the shadow of a female whom his heart had told him was Rosalie.

He had a mind to go over and see her, but, with the timidity of a lover, he feared intruding. Had she come out whilst he stood at the window he would have gone down instantly and joined her. Perhaps that was what retained him in his position for such a length of time, for with folded arms, and brows bent with thought, he stood gazing down upon the street for many minutes.

But then he was also thinking, and to a lover nothing can be more provocative of thought than the darkness of night and the nearness of the loved one. But was he thinking of her? Indirectly. She was the source from which the river of his thoughts flowed, but which as it flowed further away increased its dimensions and darted off into innumerable branches; yet all owing their birth to, all connected with, the one first fount.

His mind had got upon the subject of the gambling-house in the Rue Antoine Sarbotière, and he was wondering whether the hunchback were likely to meet with success. Then he thought of his thousand francs, and how it was only a drop in the bowl which he knew must be filled ere he could claim the girl from whom his thoughts now were hardly ever absent. But his future—what did *that* promise? He had commenced literature, and with what result? He had already tasted the bitterness of disappointment, and that draught was but a presage of the many more he should be compelled to swallow ere even a smile from the goddess he wooed might illumine the blackness of the pursuit to which he had devoted himself. How many years would he have to wait ere his least sanguine hope might be gratified, and meanwhile what would be his position? He shuddered to think, and turned as if for relief to the other picture which his imagination was holding up before him.

But it is the curse of the human mind to paint in the darkest colours that which it spontaneously rejects; whilst that to which it inclines it portrays with the soft yet brilliant light which hope can alone impart.

The gambling-house was his only refuge. So at least he thought. Yet not so much a refuge as a gate through which he had to pass before he could attain to that state which he now saw only at a distance. On this side of it were oppression, poverty, desolation, perhaps suicide; beyond were placed his love, his hope, his gladness—in a word, all that life had to supply him of what he longed for, almost wept for.

He was in the Inferno: Purgatory had to be passed before Paradise could be reached.

Thus thinking, he stood at his window until the night had blackened around him, and half-past nine sounded on the air. He started, and turning round, seized his hat and went downstairs. He paused a moment before Rosalie's house, and, throwing his hands up in the direction of the window, muttered some confused, inarticulate appeal; then, pulling his hat over his forehead, he stalked off in the direction of the Rue Antoine Sarbotière.

The room devoted to the roulette-table was full, for it was late, and the cries, shouts, and laughter of the assembled company were terribly confusing. He recognised amidst the crowd several faces which he had before noticed, but the hunchback was invisible. He almost hoped that he might have left, as he knew Sloman would attribute his presence there to a love of gambling rather than to his real motive, of which he by no means desired to enter into the explanation.

But the noise was so incessant, the atmosphere so stifling, the crowd so excited, that in order to escape the tumult and the heat, and •perhaps impelled by the recollection of his former luck in the same apartment, he pushed open the green baize door, and entered the *rouge-et-noir* room.

The first person he saw was Sloman, who was standing near the croupier, and who, upon his entrance, immediately looked up and nodded.

"I fancied you'd come," he exclaimed, making room for the young man beside him; "it's dull by one's self at home; at least when you know that there is such a place as this not far off."

"Have you been playing?"

"Yes."

"Any luck?"

"Two napoleons, that's all. I was a winner half an hour ago of sixteen, but they've settled into the miserable number I've named."

After a little while Sloman urged Williams to try his fortune. "This time, if I were you, I'd try the black."

Williams did so, and lost. "I'll stick to the red: it is my colour, after all, or I'm much mistaken," he exclaimed.

"Nonsense! don't you remember you lost upon the red last time for the first shot?"

"True. I'll try black again."

But he also lost.

"There!" he exclaimed, pettishly; "I knew red was my colour. Now then, monsieur, *rouge* this time, if you please."

He played upon the *rouge* and lost.

"Luck's against you, monsieur," said a man from the other side of the table; "give it up."

"Who spoke to you, sir?" cried Sloman, angrily.

"I was not addressing you: my remark was meant for your friend."

"Which applies equally to me. We both

know our business, and we have no need of your advice."

"Wasn't that said exactly like Father Schorchells?" said somebody to the man who had spoken.

"Hang Father Schorchells!" half shrieked Sloman. "If you annoy me any more, I'll give you in charge."

There was a burst of laughter, and a voice cried, "*Vive monsieur le bossu!*"

Sloman trembled with rage, and addressed some words to the croupier, who answered with a shrug of the shoulders that entirely hid the ears.

"Do not mind them," exclaimed Williams. "It's what they call banter, and you must submit to it. I have lost two pounds fifteen."

"That is because you have deserted the red."

Williams angrily backed the black and lost. Sloman seized him by the arm. "Give it up," said he; "fortune's against you."

"I won't," answered Williams, biting his lip until it was bloodless. "Fortune shan't master me!" Then, turning to the croupier, he cried, "Two napoleons on black!"

"You are mad!" exclaimed Sloman. "What's the use of staking so high?"

"Let go!" angrily said Williams, shaking off the hunchback's grasp. "I know what I am about. Let go. Yes, I play." This to the croupier, who was looking up at him with an inquiring glance.

The card was thrown up. It was red. Williams's face was pale, with a stifled passion; this continuance of ill-luck was maddening. Again he backed the black. Again the card turned up red.

A murmur of pity broke from the lips of the assembled company. Inured as they were to scenes of woe, they could not contemplate without an expression of sympathy, the suffering that the "jeune Anglais," seemed undergoing.

"Take your friend away, Father Schorchells," cried a voice.

Sloman, who well knew this was addressed to him, made no reply.

It needed not this request to incite him to the act, as we have seen; but there was something in the appearance of Williams that restrained him. The young man's face wore that determined expression which not only prohibits, but threatens, intervention.

"I could swear," muttered the hunchback,

"that Frank Hamilton stands before me. The likeness is marvellous."

Williams continued the game in silence, but with the same result. At last he beckoned to Sloman.

" Can you lend me five napoleons? " he hoarsely whispered.

Sloman shrugged his shoulders. "On my word, they have cleared me of what I have. But why not stop now? It is ridiculous. You will be ruined."

" Never mind—a napoleon will do. One—have you one? "

" Not even a franc."

This was a falsehood, but evidently designed to induce his friend to leave the room. It seemed to have the desired effect, for after a moment's pause, the young man snatched up his hat and disappeared.

" I'm glad he's gone," thought Sloman, " now I can play quietly. Moreover, luck is against him, and——" an idea seemed to dart across his mind, and he smiled with much apparent satisfaction. Then approaching the table he commenced betting.

A quarter of an hour after Williams had left

the room, to the profound amazement of Sloman he returned. He was reeking with perspiration, and panting as if from recent violent exercise.

" Why, what's the matter?" asked Sloman.

But without replying, the young man pushed his way to the table, and proceeded to stake a five-pound note on red. Sloman instantly comprehended that he must have been home to provide himself with more money. Anxious to watch his friend, he ceased his betting, and stood silently regarding him, together with the others, whose pity for the young man's ill-luck was now changed into contempt at his temerity. This is one of the few acts of daring that men despise.

His return seemed to have interrupted the tide of his ill-success, for the first throw was in his favour. A momentary hope inspired him that he was about to recover his losses. But Fortune in such matters is a syren who smiles but to seduce and ruin. Allured by his success, Williams renewed his stakes in heavier amounts, and in a quarter of an hour from the moment of his entry he was without a penny in his pocket.

He had been too much agitated when he came in to notice that Sloman was at the table betting, and taking him at his word that he " was cleared out," he passed silently through the crowd, and made his way into the street. The extraordinary excitement under which he had been labouring now gave way, his emotions choked his heart, and bowing his head in his hands he burst into tears.

A hand was laid upon his shoulders, and looking around, he perceived Sloman at his side.

"What is the matter with you?" asked the hunchback.

Ashamed at being discovered in his weakness, the young man coloured up to the forehead, and in a hoarse whisper answered, "I am ruined!"

"Everything gone?"

"I have not a fraction left in the world."

Sloman was too much a man of the world to tell him now in his present frame of mind that he should "have taken his advice," but silently passing his arm through his companion's, he gently led him away.

"I can respect your grief," he said, after a little; "but it will not do to give way to it. Have you no money left?"

"Not any."

"Then you have lost your thousand francs? Bah! to-morrow you will recover it."

"My thousand francs; that is nothing. I tell you I have lost every penny I had in the world."

"That is bad. However, I can assist you. I have still a little left; enough at least to rear upon it a colossal fortune."

"Will you lend me some?"

"I will."

Williams pressed the hunchback's hand in silence.

"And now," said Sloman, "the rule of gambling is this: when money is lost it must be forgotten. The memory must dismiss it as a thing that never had an existence. This is how you must treat your loss."

"I will: do not let us discuss it. It was—it was—" the young man paused, and clutched his throbbing forehead in his hands.

"It was what?"

"No matter. *Ce n'est que le premier pas qui coute.* I shall be better after this."

"Now you talk like a man."

"To-morrow evening I will break the bank. I feel it here," and the young man violently tapped his breast.

Ah! he still trusted to his presentiments. Had

he so soon forgotten Mr. Brown—his own disappointment?

" So you shall," said Sloman, tapping him upon
the back.

" None but the brave, none but the brave, none
but the brave deserve—success. Now I think
that quotation apt."

Williams tried to force a laugh at the hunchback's joke. The strange influence which that
man exercised over all those who came in imme-
diate contact with him was now beginning to be
felt by his young companion. It was the old
simile of the basilisk charming the transfixed bird,
renewed and embodied. Though his heart was
nearly breaking, this influence compelled from
him a laugh at his companion's joke. It was
hollow, it was mocking, but it was a tacit acqui-
escence in Sloman's superiority. So the trembling
schoolboy palely smiles at the joke of the usher
whose cane is uplifted over the little, extended
hand.

CHAPTER IX.

A CURIOUS RESOLUTION.

THE excitement of the previous evening, his violent emotions, his passion, his despair, had left traces of their conflict visible in Williams's face, for when he arose the next morning it seemed as if he had suddenly grown old in the night, so haggard was the expression on his features, so pale his cheeks, so restless his eyes.

It was undoubtedly a terrible blow for the young man. The enchanter, Hope, had built before him a gorgeous pile, emblazoned with every beauty of promise, of fortune, of success, but at one stroke of the wand of the wizard Fate, the magnificence had toppled into bleak reality, leaving in its room a cold memory to impart not pleasure but despair, and to render more bitter the present by contrasting it with that which had preceded it.

He descended the stairs, and knocked at Sloman's door.

"Come in," cried the hunchback.

Williams entered, and found the hunchback still in bed. This was a spectacle he had not before seen, and at which, therefore, he felt strongly inclined to laugh, in spite of his feelings, which were of anything but of a mirthful complexion. But the truth was, Mr. Sloman had pulled over his head, as far as his eyebrows, a flannel nightcap, which, either inflated by air, or naturally stiff, shot up in a point, thereby lending to the owner's face an aspect as ridiculous as can be well imagined.

"Well, and what sort of a night did you pass?" asked Sloman.

Williams shook his head. "Such a night," he answered, "as I could suppose a man would pass who lay distended for the twelve hours upon a rack. But I have come to ask you to oblige me. I have not a penny in my pocket. Can you supply me with a little money until the evening?"

"How much do you want?"

"What can you spare?"

"Will five napoleons do you?"

"Very well indeed."

"Feel in that waistcoat pocket hanging up there, and you'll find the money."

Williams did so, and turning to Sloman, said, " I am deeply indebted to you for this."

" Quite welcome, quite welcome ! " replied Sloman; " mind you pay me back again when you have it."

" Most assuredly. I am going out for a little. My head is hot, and the cool of the morning may ease me."

" Good ; and I shall sleep for another two hours."

Williams went downstairs, and into the street. Just as he had closed his own door behind, the door opposite opened, and Rosalie came out ; she uttered an exclamation of surprise, and ran across the road.

" Why', Mr. Williams, this is an unexpected meeting ! Who would have thought of meeting you here so early in the morning ? "

" I live there, now," said Williams, pointing to the house. " You see we are close neighbours."

She was about to make some remark, but checking herself, she blushed deeply, and bowed her head a little. She thought that he had come expressly to be near her, and this fancy, whilst it had brought the blush to her' cheek, restrained the question she was about to ask—what brought him there?

Perhaps he interpreted her silence, for he said in a low voice, " My change was sudden, but—but—many things prompted it, you amongst the chief."

" I?"

" I wanted to be near you. I was lonely where I lived before. My only companion had died, and—and—to be friendless in a large city is very terrible, Mademoiselle Gautier."

She looked at him earnestly for awhile, and then said, hurriedly, " Are you not well?"

" Perfectly well. Why do you ask me?"

" Your face wears a look of suffering; it is pale, and somewhat thinner since I last saw you."

He pressed his hand to his heart, as if to stifle there a sudden pain; then, with a forced smile, he said, " I am growing old, Mademoiselle Gautier."

But the penetration of a woman was not to be baffled by a mask so pitiful as this; she saw at a glance that he was ill, nay, was suffering from a something more than mere bodily illness; but she saw also that he wished to conceal his feelings, whatever they might be, and she quietly changed the subject.

" I have to go as far as the Rue ——. Where is your destination ? "

" Nowhere; or rather, anywhere. May I accompany you ? "

She gracefully smiled back her reply, and then glancing up at her father's house, she walked away by the side of her lover.

She asked him a number of questions as to the reasons of his movements, and he replied by acquainting her of the death of Mr. Brown; his legacy, and his disappointment.

" And what are you doing now, Mr. Williams ? "

He faintly blushed as he replied, " Working always."

" Still writing, I suppose ? "

A doubtful nod of the head was his only answer, and then he abruptly asked her if she knew the hunchback who resided in the same house with him.

" No; but I have seen him once only; and that was in the street, as I met you just now. Poor man ! such deformity as his must be a dreadful calamity."

" Dreadful indeed. I have recently made his acquaintance, and let me assure you his voice and conversation are hardly less grotesque than his appearance."

" Are you going to remain in Paris long? " she asked him, after a little.

" My future is very uncertain. I know not what I may do."

There was a pause, and then he whispered hurriedly, " If I leave it, it shall be starvation alone that drives me from it."

"Starvation !" she asked, with a start.

" Better men than I have starved," he muttered, gloomily.

She shook her head at him, and feigned a light smile. " You are frightening me," she whispered; " you are not in earnest."

He seized her hand, and grasped it in silence for a moment; then letting it fall, he murmured, " Ah, Mademoiselle Gautier, it will be a cruel necessity that compels me to separate myself from you."

She blushed, but without evading his glance. " What necessity is it that you anticipate ? " she inquired.

" It matters not. I am strong—I am young—

I have hope. These three incitements may, perhaps, assist me to a purpose and to an end."

"You will often come in and see us now?" she said; "you are so near, and you can find no excuse to remain away."

"Excuse to remain away! Ah, I fear that I should rather need apologies for my constant intrusion."

"Not yet, at any rate," she answered, a little poutingly; "you have only given us the pleasure of your society once; and as I know you do not object to my father's eccentric mode of welcoming his guests, you can really frame no plea to excuse your absence."

"A thousand thanks for your goodness. After what you have said, I shall now begin to infest you."

"Do. I can, at least, assure you a welcome. And selfishly, your presence really confers a boon upon us, for it is dull at home of an evening." And Rosalie sighed.

It was astonishing the effect of this girl's presence on the mind of the young man. It was like a sunbeam illumining some dark recess, and driving from it the shadows that obscured it. Insensibly he felt himself cheered by her conversation, though it mattered not of what nature it partook. The sweet sounds of her voice thrilled him through with that unspeakable feeling which is always begotten by the tones of a cherished friend; a feeling now rendered doubly pleasurable, since to the purity of friendship was united the softness, the beauty of love.

They walked on together, Rosalie artfully varying the conversation so as to lead him to forget the cause of his distress; for that he was suffering, and that this suffering was owing to a cause which he was anxious to conceal, she had from the commencement perceived; she had all the curiosity to divine it, from the true wish to impart, if possible, her little mite of comfort; but whilst her delicacy forbade her inquiring, her sympathy and her tact sought to direct the conversation to a channel the most likely to divert him from the remembrance of that *something* in his heart of which she too plainly perceived the existence.

On parting, she said to him, " Do come in this evening and see us ?"

He hesitated, and mumbled a trust that she would excuse him, and so forth.

" I will admit of no excuse. You must come.

Why, what have you got in particular to do to-night?"

" Nothing—nothing much."

" Then why won't you come?"

She had asked him out of pure kindness, think-ing he might be dull and lonely by himself in his apartments.   He had hesitated to accept her invi-tation, because he remembered the Rue Antoine Sarbotière, and the fortune that he had sworn to retrieve that evening.   But he remembered he could visit it later, after he should have left the Gautiers; and so he replied, "I will do myself then the pleasure of seeing you.   But will not M. Gautier consider me an intruder?"

" Not in heart, whatever his conduct may demonstrate.   Do not misunderstand papa," she said, assuming a cheerful voice, " he is much better than he may appear."

He pressed his lips to her hand, and they separated.

He would not tell Sloman of his proposed visit, but on that worthy's asking him if he intended making his appearance at the gambling-house, he answered—

"Yes; but not until late.   I have promised myself luck, and mean to lay this night the foundations of a fortune upon your five napoleons."

"Well, I hope you will," said Sloman. "By the way," he added, after a pause, "if ever we should grow ' hard-up,' you could always find assistance in your old friend opposite, couldn't you?"

"In M. Gautier?"

"Yes."

Williams shook his head. "He is a miser," he said; "it is not likely that he would advance me five sous unless I could procure and provide him with good securities."

"But still you might try him."

"My friend, I love the daughter; I could not, would not degrade myself in *her* eyes by stooping to solicit such assistance from her father."

A shade of disappointment passed across the hunchback's face, and he beat his foot noisily against the ground,—a certain sign of his irritability.

"If you are going to allow your pride to interfere with your interests," he exclaimed, "adieu to fortune. That's all I have to say."

"Well, do not let us quarrel about the matter yet. Thanks to your generosity, these five napo-

leons may place me in a position completely independent of the old man."

" Well, I hope it may !" and sullenly turning
upon his heel the hunchback descended to his
own apartments. Williams did not choose to
notice his companion's manner. His liberality in
the morning had disarmed him of whatever re-
sentment such conduct as this might otherwise
have provoked. Sloman's suggestion was, however, by no means one likely to be adopted by the
young man. He had, it is true, plainly told
Rosalie of his poverty; but rather than sue her
father, or even that she should know the pressing
exigences of his position, he would have stooped
to a crime, and at the expense of his conscience
achieved what his pride prohibited him to sup-
plicate.

Such are the contradictions of human nature,
and such that startling paradox, the human heart !

He had not become old enough, or reflective, to
weigh the motives of men's conduct, and to pursue
their designs through the ramifications of their
self-interest, else the simple questions that had
otherwise infallibly occurred,—" Why the reason
of Mr. Sloman's apparent solicitude in my welfare
—his desire for my companionship—his willing

assistance in the hour of need?"—must have excited his curiosity and tempted him into conjecture or inquiry. That Sloman had a motive in all that he did my reader has long since found out; and though the cause was frequently very inadequate to the effect—though, like the genius in the box found by the fisherman, from the least possible reason a tremendous result was evoked; he nevertheless took the same precaution, exercised the same skill, practised the same conduct, and weighed each probability with the same precision that would have done credit to the minister upon whom dexterity of achieving his ends might have depended the fate of an empire.

On leaving the house Williams told Sloman that he might expect to see him at the Rue Antoine Sarbotière at about ten o'clock.

"And what are you going to do in the meantime?" asked Sloman.

"Well, to tell you the truth, I have made an appointment which I am anxious to keep."

"All right."

It was dark in the street, and the hunchback could not see him cross; nevertheless he flattened his cheek against the window in order to discern, if possible, whether his friend took the turning at the bottom of the road, or went straight on. As he did neither, but simply crossed over to the other side, Sloman of course saw nothing, and with a grunt he threw himself into a chair, and rang for lights.

The door was opened to Williams by old Gautier, who this time held a light in his hand.

"Well, Mr. Freddy," he said, "and how are you? Come in—come in!"

"Am I an intruder, M. Gautier?"

"No, no! Have you had tea?"

Williams could hardly forbear a smile as he answered,—"No."

"Ah!" sighed M. Gautier, "very well; by and by Rosalie shall make you a cup."

"Is that your office?" asked Williams, pointing to a glass-door in the passage.

"Yes," said M. Gautier, "that is my office; would you like to see it?"

"I should."

M. Gautier, holding the candle over his head, pushed the door open and entered. It was an ordinary office, with a little table in the centre and a few chairs arranged around. A padlocked ledger stood upon the mantelpiece, and in the corner was a small iron safe.

"That's the bank, I suppose?" said Williams, pointing to the safe.

M. Gautier glanced out of the corner of his eyes at Williams, and shook his head.

"A very poor bank," said he.

"I wonder you allow it to stand here all night; are you not afraid of a robbery?"

Old Gautier trembled as he answered,—

"I am! and that's just what Rosalie can't understand. But you can, though."

"Of course I can. If that safe contains money, I do not think you are right in leaving it in a position so exposed."

"Ah, but," said the old man, with a cunning wink of the eye, "it wants a skilful thief to open it, for the lock is a patent one. Just hear the click of it," and drawing a key from his pocket he applied it to the lock, which turned with a loud noise indicating its strength.

"You mean the lock is powerful, but not patent," said Williams.

"Well, isn't that patent? What robber could break it open? But," said M. Gautier, approaching Williams, and taking his arm, "it isn't left down here all night, you know; I take it upstairs," he added in a kind of mysterious whisper,

"and nobody would dare attempt to rob it there."
Then shaking his head as if to contradict a supposition that had entered his mind, he let fall his companion's arm, and continued: "Pooh, pooh! but there's very little to rob in it, Mr. Williams. Aha! only papers, deeds, and so forth; and who wants them, eh? Aha!"

"True," said Williams, anxious to humour the old man, "they are of no use to anybody but the possessor."

"Exactly, exactly. Ah, dear sir, will you do me a very great favour? it will save my girl the job, as she and I usually perform it; will you lend me a hand to convey the safe upstairs?"

"With the greatest possible pleasure."

"Thank you," said the old man, bustling about; "thank you. Now, then, this is how I generally manage it." And leaving the room, he shortly after reappeared, bearing a small stretcher, which he placed upon the ground. "Now, if you will help me to place the safe upon that thing, we'll be able to carry it up as easily as possible. You take this end, and I'll take that." And with some groans from the old man, who displayed considerable strength for his years, and with some little straining on the part of Williams, the safe was raised and placed upon the stretcher. Then M. Gautier seized some cords and commenced binding it down.

Williams could not help thinking that if the safe contained only papers, those papers were uncommonly heavy. But he made no remark.

Grasping each man one end of the stretcher, they proceeded upstairs, Williams taking the lead and mounting backwards. The old man below him perspired considerably over the labour; but he seemed quite to enjoy it, ever and anon urging Williams to be a little less vehement, and not to go quite so fast. At the top of the landing Rosalie came out of the room, anxious to know the cause of the tumult.

"Oh, papa!" she exclaimed, catching a sight at once of Williams's back making at her, and her father's head jerking slowly upstairs below after him, "what a shame to be sure to give Mr. Williams all this trouble!"

"Not at all," said Williams, who was red in the face with his exertion: but who could not turn his head to look at her. "On the contrary, it is quite a pleasure."

"I am sure he likes it!" cried the old man; "why, it's capital exercise. In that room, please," he said, when they had reached the landing.

Rosalie opened the door for them to pass through, and, after some further labour, the safe was deposited in a corner of the apartment.

"There!" said M. Gautier, panting and eying his property with much satisfaction, "Mr. Williams has saved you a job to-night, Rosalie."

"Is it possible, Mam'selle Gautier, that you can find strength enough to carry that heavy box upstairs?" asked Williams.

"He calls it heavy!" interrupted old Gautier; "why, what would it be if it were full of coin, instead of useless papers?" A significant glance from Rosalie confirmed Williams, however, in his first suspicions that there was something more than paper secreted in M. Gautier's iron safe.

"We manage it somehow or other, don't we, papa?" said Rosalie, in reply to Williams's question.

"Yes, every night of our lives, excepting Sundays."

"Then," said Williams, "you must permit me to congratulate you upon your really Amazonian strength."

Rosalie laughed, and old Gautier asked what

Amazonian meant, whereupon a little amiable squabble took place between the young couple as to who should explain. It was at length resolved that Rosalie should do so; and this she did, very prettily; actually quoting, to the amazement and delight of Williams, an erudite author, who had written a learned work on the origin, progress, and decline of the Nation of Amazons. M. Gautier eyed his daughter with pride, ever and anon casting a glance at Williams, to see what effect all this learning had upon him.

The industry of the young man had evidently operated beneficially upon the mind of the old, for after a little he turned to his daughter and bade her procure the visitor some tea. Rosalie smiled as she passed Williams, who comprehended her meaning, and faintly nodded back a reply.

As in the morning, so now the presence of Rosalie dissipated the oppression of the young man's heart, and during the hours that he spent with her, he thought once or twice only of the gambling-house and his companion Sloman.

A little while before he left, Rosalie said to him, "Mr. Williams, has it never entered your mind to try and discover your origin, who your parents were, and whether they are still living?"

"I have often thought of it," answered Williams, sadly; "but what would be the use of my attempting to search out the past? If my parents are living, it is evident they do not want me, otherwise they would not have deserted me as an infant. If they are dead, the discovery would be useless to me."

"But have you no anxiety to learn about the past? Surely you must have relations living in the world who could furnish you with all the information you require."

" Relations ! " exclaimed Williams, bitterly; "I only knew one, and after years of harsh treatment, she at last spurned me from her door, to seek an asylum under the roof of one of those cold-hearted tyrants, one of those low wretches, whom God creates and sends upon earth merely that the proud and the vain-glorious may look upon them and remember that they are men ! "

"But you may have others who are better hearted, who are kind, generous ?"

"Mam'selle Gautier, we have an old, homely, but true proverb in our language, which says that 'a burnt child dreads the fire.' Even at this distance of time I cannot recall, without a blush of indignation, the unnatural, the cruel, the almost outrageous treatment to which I was subject as a child : not so much from the stranger, who was but an instrument in the hands of another, as from her to whom I was united by the ties of blood, in whom my helplessness should have found protection, even if my relationship were not entitled to her kindness. Relations! No. I would rather battle through the world in poverty and obscurity—battle through it as I *am*, —than owe one obligation to those who deserted or neglected me as a child, and have since utterly ignored my existence ! "

" I cannot blame you," replied Rosalie, in a low voice. " But, living or dead, do not condemn your parents until you have become better acquainted with their history. Rather attribute your calamities to those you know than to those you have never seen."

" I will try: but my resolutions can matter little. Too many years have flown that I should ever hope to have even the faintest memorial of the past restored to me. If my parents are dead, God rest their souls! Their son can breathe no other prayer. They left me like a waif upon the ocean of life to be tossed to and fro at the mercy of strangers. Young as I am, I have known but little happiness. I have gone through the world alone—almost desolate. I have met with many frowns, but few smiles. One friend only have I made—Rosalie, it is you!"

He took her hand and pressed it fondly to his lips, and at the same moment the tones of a clock striking in the distance fell upon his ear.

"It is ten!" he cried, suddenly starting. "I must go. Farewell!"

"What is your hurry?"

He hesitated, and at length said, "An important engagement."

"Then I will not detain you. Adieu!"

"Your father is asleep. Do not let me disturb him."

"You must often come to us now," said Rosalie, in a sweet, low voice; "you are so near: and we are so glad to see you."

"Trust me, I shall often see you! Farewell." And kissing his hand to her, he left the apartment.

He had some little difficulty in getting out, as the door was locked. The bolts grated hoarsely as he pushed them back, and slamming the door heavily after him, that the noise might awaken old Gautier, who would be sure to descend and

drive the bolts to again, he made his way thoughtfully in the direction of the Rue Antoine Sarbotière.

*   *   *   *

*   *   *   *

Three hours after this, namely, at one o'clock
in the morning, a man was walking in the direction of the Rue Colville by himself. It was a
cold night; and a quarter-moon, of that colour
which belongs rather to the wintry nights of
January than the more tempered skies of October,
indicated the presence of a bleak wind. The
man seemed to feel it, for he hugged himself
tightly across the breast, and trod forward with a
rapid though irregular motion. His face was
deadly pale, and his lips moved in the articu-
lation of an incoherent conversation he was holding with himself. Sometimes he paused and
thrust his hands in his pockets; then withdraw-
ing them with a murmur of despair, he clasped
them again across his breast and hurried on.

At last he entered the Rue Colville, and
here again he stopped. This time his eyes were
fixed upon a house opposite, and he stood for a
long while motionlessly regarding it. A terrible
expression of despair was upon his face, and ever

and anon he would grind his teeth with a violence that would have startled any passenger who
might have been passing at the moment. All the
while he continued talking to himself—not in the
noisy accent of an enraged man, but with that
determined, terrible tone which may be heard
murmuring from the lips of the suicide as he
glides by you in the street towards his self-
prepared doom.

At last he turned abruptly on his heel, and
opening a door with a latch-key which he produced from his pocket, he slammed it violently to
after him, and glided upstairs. On reaching the
second landing he tapped at a door, and the voice
of Sloman from within, cried:

" Who's there ? "

" May I come in ? "

" Hallo ! is it you, Williams ? Yes, come
along."

Williams—for it was he—thrust the door open,
and entered the apartment. Sloman uttered an
exclamation of alarm as his eye encountered the
form of his friend.

" Why," he cried, " what have you been doing
to yourself ? "

Williams made a gesture to command silence,

and approching a little grate in which yet glowed
the remains of a recent fire, he muttered :

"I am cold."

The hunchback eyed him for a moment without remark; then turning to the table, he poured
out half a glass of cognac from a bottle and
handed it to his companion.

"That will warm you," he said.

Williams seized the tumbler and emptied the
fiery contents at a draught. This seemed to
revive him, for after a few moments he looked up
and said :

"I thought to find you dead."

"Why?" asked the hunchback, without testify-
ing any surprise at the curious remark.

"Have you not lost everything ?"

"No."

"You told me you had."

"True. I forgot at that moment that I had
five napoleons remaining."

"Fool!" cried Williams, impetuously; "why
didn't you play them? You might have re-
covered them all."

Sloman shrugged his shoulders.

"My reason for not playing them was—my
benevolence."

"Cease this banter!" exclaimed Williams, his two hands outspread before, and his face presenting a weird appearance in the glow of the dying embers. "You will drive me crazy. Talk —talk—sensibly. Do you not see my mood?" He turned his face to Sloman, and glared at him from beneath his contracted eyebrows.

"Pooh! I am as badly off as you, yet you see I can control myself. You are a novice— therefore I forgive you."

There was a silence, and then Williams said:

"Why didn't you play the five napoleons?"

"I have told you."

"Repeat your reason."

"Because I am benevolent."

This coolness was evidently maddening to Williams: he leapt to his feet, and commenced violently pacing the room.

"Come," continued Sloman, "you appear to want to know the reason, and I'll give it you. My motive for not playing my five napoleons was this: you had them, and I had not the heart to ask you for them."

With a half shriek of rage, Williams turned upon him.

"I am ruined: your money is gone—you saw

it go! How could you ask me? Would you have wanted them in drops of blood? Gone, I say! I hadn't them to pay you. You were near me. You saw me fling down the last—the last upon the red : and it went."

"Then I left."

"I saw you go. But what cared I? Look! I came here freezing. Shall I tell you why? I searched my pockets for more money—they were empty. I was poor—I had no jewelry about me. I tore off my cloak and offered it to the croupier as a stake. The wretch laughed at me, and turned around as if to procure assistance— for he seemed frightened. He refused me two francs for my cloak—for my cloak worth twenty! I offered it to the crowd around the table, and for awhile they also laughed at me. Then some one cried, 'I will take it.' I held it out to him and received the money. I was mad—crazed with my recent loss, and thought that I might perhaps retrieve the whole with a two-franc piece. Such things have been, man—nay, do not laugh at me! I know such things have been, I——"

"And what became of your two francs? "

"Gone!"

The rapid manner in which he had detailed his

first speech, whilst it had rendered his delivery almost incoherent, had also made him breathless. He gasped rather than said "gone," and then, clutching the back of a chair, fell almost fainting into it.

But the hunchback betrayed no emotion whatever at his companion's distress; on the contrary, he sat cool and collected, and spoke quite dispassionately when he said:

"Gone, eh? And with it, I suppose, my five napoleons?"

"You shall be paid," muttered Williams, "even if I have to beg for it."

"Do not think, my friend, that I wish to compel you into payment. On the contrary, I would willingly forgive you the debt; but," he continued, assuming a whining voice, "you see my position. I too am ruined. Your fatal luck has pursued me equally with yourself."

Williams remained silent, and Sloman continued:

"Look you! if you could only contrive to become possessed of a little money, just to start us both again, I would gladly forego all recollection of the debt of five napoleons, and accept a portion of it as a gift. Indeed, money must be got some way or other; else we shall starve."

A terrible conflict seemed to be going on in Williams's breast, for his clenched fist was convulsively jerking about, and his lips were moving with a strange, wild rapidity. Sloman watched him for awhile in silence, and then exclaimed:

"Wouldn't your friend Gautier assist you if you were to appeal to him?"

Something in the hunchback's speech appeared to have penetrated a vital part, for suddenly leaping to his feet, Williams went over to his companion and grasped him almost painfully by the arm.

"You are right," he hoarsely exclaimed; "this Gautier shall assist me—but not voluntarily, for that he would not do. He is a miser, and would spurn me from him if I begged. Beg—no!—I could not do that—and *she* to know it."

"Let go my arm," said Sloman; "seat yourself and talk the matter calmly over."

But Williams still retained his grasp, and in the same violent manner continued:

"We must have money—you say so—and you are right. Where am I to get it—where go for it? I am friendless—so are you. We must turn thieves, man, and rob!"

He almost hissed the last words, and releasing his grasp of Sloman's arm, stood upright before him.

"As you will," said the hunchback, coolly; "show me the booty, and I will help you to secure it."

"A little would do—we do not want much. We could repay it when we discovered ourselves to be winners."

"Of course we could. Fortunes are made by degrees: but they want a beginning. Where are we to find ours?"

"There!" Williams was pointing with his finger in the direction of the window.

"In M. Gautier's house?"

A nod was his answer.

"But if he is a miser, he has coffers; and how are those coffers to be opened?"

Williams uttered a loud, terrible laugh. "His coffers are an iron-safe! A safe heavy with gold. I helped him to carry it up to his room only a few hours ago."

Sloman bent eagerly forward, and fixed his gleaming eyes on his companion's face.

"Have you the key to this safe?" he inquired.

Williams shook his head.

"But it is easily procured," he said. "Besides we only want a little—just a little, my friend, to help us to live—to save us from starvation. He would not miss it; and—and—we would repay him tenfold when luck favoured us."

"Ay, that we would. But we must have money, Williams; else we starve."

"We starve! Let us starve; will we not be happier dead?"

"Bosh! Death comes quite quickly enough. It is the business of the living to learn how to live, not to think how to die."

"Why shouldn't it be done. *She* would pardon me, if she knew all. It is for her; I might claim her then. But to beg from her father—to be spurned, perhaps, from his door—oh, never! And a little, too—just a little: and so easily repaid— ten-times repaid; ay, twenty-times!" His language was evidently addressed to himself, and not to the hunchback who sat listening to him. It seemed as if he were striving to self-exonerate himself from his meditated conduct.

"Fortify your determination with this!" exclaimed Sloman, emptying the remaining contents of the brandy-bottle into a tumbler, and offering it to Williams. "Money must be procured; that is certain. With it, though only a little, we may beat Fortune, and compel her favours in spite of herself; and then let your own imagination supply you with the happiness such a fortune would give you. But without it——," he shrugged his shoulders, and fixed his eye upon the face of his companion.

"But it is to be had—and shall be!" cried Williams, who refused to accept the brandy which Sloman offered him. "Dishonourably? What matters? Must we perish like dogs, with plenty within our reach? Dishonour! It is an empty word to the hungry stomach—to the broken-hearted man; to the dreamer whose dreams are shattered and dissipated! Honour—dishonour; they are alike to me. Food must be had for the present; money must be made for the future. There is no longer honour or dishonour in the world. There is beggary—want—starvation! I must have money! It is *there!* and we will procure it!"

"Good! Invent your own scheme, and when ready, here's the man to assist you." And Sloman tapped himself upon the breast.

"He has a safe, you know. What is easier than to forge a key?"

"Nothing."

"We might enter his house at night. I will find the means. The safe is in his sitting-room. He sleeps on the floor above. We must move silently, friend, silently! A noise would frighten him, and then—the discovery! Twenty pounds would do us. We would give him by-and-by a hundred for his loan."

"But why not first strive to borrow it?"

"I tell you it would be useless. He is a miser; man, do you know what a miser means?"

"Perfectly."

"I'll stoop to the crime, but not to the degradation his refusal would put upon me. It would bar me for ever from his daughter. He would prohibit me the house. But to take from his safe, in the dead of night—he would not know the thief: perhaps, think it his own mistake."

"Your logic is admirable. I leave the matter to you. First, invent your scheme, then include me."

There came a long silence, and Williams, treading on tip-toe towards the window, looked out on to the opposite house. The hunchback did not turn to notice him, but sat with folded hands and a smile upon his face, as if he had now realised his expectations—now achieved what he had laboriously sought to win. Suddenly Williams turned to him. " How are we to live," he asked, " for to-morrow, perhaps the next day ? "

After a little hesitation, Sloman put his hand in his pocket, and extracted a napoleon, which he held up. At the sight of this, Williams furiously rushed across the room to him, and grasping him by the hand, gazed for a short while speechless upon the coin it contained. " Why did you not tell me you had this ? " he fiercely exclaimed at last; " why did you not lend it me, or stake it yourself. It might have changed the tide of fortune ; saved us from want, degradation, crime ! "

" You see," said Sloman, rising from his chair, and placing himself before the fire-place, " my misfortune is that I can't get you to talk reasonably. You ask me why I didn't lend you this before; now if I had, should we have possessed it to purchase food with to-morrow ? It might have brought us luck—but then also, it mightn't ; and if it hadn't, we should have wanted bread. So rather than leave ourselves wholly in the hands of fortune, I secreted this; and I think I am right."

"We did not want bread for the morrow: we wanted money for this night," answered Williams, gloomily. Then, striking his clenched fist against the palm of his other hand, he muttered, "It might have saved us."

At this moment a church-clock commenced striking. The hunchback held up his finger, and counted the strokes. "One, two, three. Three o'clock. Humph! Let us get to bed. In the daylight mature your schemes, but in the night execute them!" Then, extending his hand to Williams, he exclaimed, "Keep up your spirits, man, I say! The future is yet bright before us. We have only this step to take, and fortune, seeing our determination, will let us mount the whole ladder, without opposition."

The two men clasped hands, and Williams turned upon his heel and left the apartment. But as the door closed behind, Sloman heard him say, "It might have saved us, though; it might have saved us!"

"Fool!" muttered the hunchback. "Does he think I am like him? to lose all my money at one fatal fling, and then to curse Fortune for her treachery? Bah! I knew he would be of use to me. Here have I still five hundred pounds left;—ha, ha!—and the idiot thinks me ruined. Well, to him I am. And so I'll make him support me on old Gautier's money! He shall turn thief for me, and when he fails, I can always return to my own store. He might have borrowed, if he would, but the fool has pride. And a queer pride too, so help me! that prefers robbing, like a villain, to petitioning, like a gentleman. But what is it to me? Let him continue to supply me as long as he will. He is an excellent instrument—young, and to be adapted to every purpose. And I, what am I, Sloman, that can make men so useful to thee? What must be thy cunning, thou hunchback? A Jew! Judea never boasted half so skilful a thinker. Five hundred pounds left, and he thinks me worth a single napoleon!" He chuckled to himself, making a gurgling kind of noise, as if the laugh were too delicious to escape his mouth. Then, tearing off his upper garments, he went to bed.

CHAPTER X.

THE conduct of our story compels us to take a brief glance at two personages, whom pressing events have for some time hurried out of sight.

It was evident that Belmont was not yet satisfied with his revenge on Murray; else, instead of taking him home with him to his hotel, he would have left him on the bridge, where it is possible the wretched man, maddened by the blackness of the fate with which he was surrounded, would have committed suicide. I am not sure, however, that this was Murray's design in seeking the river. His movements were mechanical, his will being overborne by his frenzy; and he had followed withersoever his footsteps chose to lead him. Nevertheless, standing alone over that black current, driven by the poignancy of his despair, and allured by the prospect of rest, it might have come to pass that in one moment of desperation, a leap would have been taken, and his own life added to the many which that river—that insatiable, devouring river —has swallowed up.

But the presence of Belmont, added to the new life imparted by his conversation, had changed the current of the man's thoughts. That hope whispered to him by his companion : that hope so dearly purchased at the loss of all that he had lived for in the present, all that he had cherished in the future, had reanimated the life in his heart, and taught him whilst this was to be achieved, to look upon death as the terror and the obstacle to his wishes that he had considered it before. To *revenge* himself upon his foe : to hunt the hunch-back Sloman out, and face to face compel him to expiate in his blood the sufferings to which he had reduced him—this was the new life that Belmont had imparted to him : this was the new hope with which Belmont had inspired him.

But in all this, Belmont himself plainly perceived a protraction of the sufferings of his victim, of which the conclusion could alone be death. So far, his scheme of revenge had succeeded in a manner that had amazed him. One blow had been followed by another with such rapidity,

that he grew at last to deem his conduct honourable.

It was with a stern, terrible pride that he surveyed the wreck of his foe, and remembered that
his fall was owing to his own machinations. The
design was certainly laboured with all the ingenuity of vengeance. It had commenced with
Murray: it should terminate with Sloman. They
seemed like puppets, in the hands of this outraged
man. They were set against each other; the
hunchback first to persecute Murray, and drive
him to the very brink of destruction; then for
Murray to turn thirsting for the blood of his foe,
and to pursue him to the death.

But the latter part of his scheme was yet to be
accomplished, and this Belmont designed when he
followed Murray to the bridge, and spoke to him
of Sloman and revenge.

So they walked back to the hotel, Belmont
conversing on the way of his plans to pursue the
hunchback, and to assist Murray to the utmost of
his power in gratifying his thirst for retribution.

He had proposed that they should start for
Paris the next day, but on his arrival home he
found a letter addressed to him from Liverpool,
requiring his presence in two days, at that town,

on matters of the greatest moment. What these matters were, the letter did not go on to state; but from the name of the writer, he understood that they were of importance, and, moreover, intimately connected with the business of the house at Hongkong, in which he had been a partner.

This greatly annoyed him, and he instantly dispatched a letter, requesting to know whether the business could not be transacted by proxy. He received a reply on the following evening in the negative, assuring him that, as his signature was wanted to an important document, he alone could attend to the summons.

It was not to be helped, and the visit to Paris was compelled to be deferred until his return. Murray chafed with impatience, and declared that by this delay Sloman might escape him.

"I have no fear of that," said Belmont. "He has your thirteen hundred pounds, and he will stop where he is, until it is gone; that is to say, if he is in Paris at all."

"He is in Paris, I know," answered Murray. "He told me he was going there; and, moreover, to prove the truth of his assertion, he showed me his passport."

"Well, if he did that, you are safe. He is in Paris, and the only difficulty will be now to get there soon. I'll engage to have him hunted out for you. The French detectives are wonderful men."

"How long are you likely to be away?"

"Perhaps two days; perhaps a week. At all events, you may depend upon my coming back as soon as ever I can."

"In your absence I will sell my furniture, and scrape together all the money I can. When my mission is over, with *him*, I shall go to Australia."

Belmont drily laughed. "A splendid field for enterprise."

"Were you ever there?"

"On the map—often."

"Ha! I shall attempt the diggings, or commence farmer."

"Both profitable, I am told. Some of these days I shall meet you again in England, a wealthy man."

"No—you'll never have me back again here. I have suffered too much in this country."

"Bah! *la maladie du pays* is a disease from which no man is exempt; an Englishman least of all. But never mind about the future; you have a present to get over that may cause you some trouble yet."

Murray's face assumed a malignant, determined expression, as he replied, "Trouble or not, it *shall* be got over.   I have sworn to pursue him through the world, and I will keep my word."

"During my absence, shall you want any assistance from me?"

"No; I have your cheque for two hundred pounds yet untouched."

"Very well."

After a little further discussion, they separated for the night.

Two days after this, Belmont started on his errand to Liverpool.   In his absence Murray remained secreted the greater part of the day, venturing out only in the evening, and then slinking along as if he dreaded to encounter the eyes of the world.   The consciousness of his guilt weighed upon his soul with the oppression of terror.   He knew not to whom Sloman might not have communicated the papers in his possession, and a constant fear now possessed him that every moment he might be apprehended by some shrewd detective employed by the other owners of the "Water Witch."   The state of his mind had been such as to render him almost forgetful of the fact that he too owned a portion of this vessel; but when he recollected it, his fear prevented him from visiting the office, to enter into any fresh negotiations; and he resolved to await the return of Belmont to offer him this share in sale, or to secure his assistance in disposing of it elsewhere.

Some days passed away without his receiving any news of Belmont. At last, one morning there came a letter from him, stating that he had been compelled to go on to Edinburgh, greatly to his annoyance, as he was excessively anxious to return. He feared that he would also have to visit Glasgow; certain merchants in these cities having entered into a partnership to purchase the business at Hongkong, which compelled his presence, for reasons which he would not weary Murray by detailing. "But keep up your spirits," he added; "everything may be for the best; and perhaps this may be only a scheme of Fortune's to render more easy the gratification of your darling wish. Be patient. True revenge is always patient. Watch the hawk in the skies, and see how motionlessly it floats in the air, waiting for the moment to dart at its victim. Be like the hawk. Not a flap of its wing reveals its presence ; let not the least impatience betray your intention. Wait until the moment comes to strike. *Then* let the blow be sure ! " The clenched hand and compressed, white lips, showed how Murray had received this advice.

One evening a longing seized this man to visit the scenes of his former happiness. He would have been there days before, but the unspeakable dread of being seen, recognised, and passed un-noticed had hitherto withheld him. He still loved Alice. Bruised as his heart had been by her in-fidelity, yet the magic of his love still exercised a wondrous influence over his thoughts. Con-stantly were they directed to her, the cause of perhaps the only pure emotion the man may have felt in his life; and the recollection served only ten-fold to embitter his present position, and to add fresh fuel to the fire of the revenge that burnt within him towards Sloman.

Indeed, as he came to review these late incidents in his life, he felt often inclined to doubt whether he were actually waking ; whether the whole were not a protracted, hideous dream, from which he would arise to find himself as he had been before. Every calamity had occurred to him with such amazing rapidity ! From his first encounter with

Belmont to the present moment, the series of blows that had befallen him, seemed, by the velocity with which they were dealt, to resemble one mighty shock, prostrating him to the dust, and leaving him powerless to act, to fly, to think. Sometimes he rubbed his eyes and gazed dully around him, murmuring to himself, with a prayer upon his lip, that the spell of slumber in which he lay enchanted, and in which he was confiued with his hideous dream, would soon be dissolved : that he might arise, and walk forth, and look upon the sun, and the sky, and men's faces, as he did in the days of yore. But even as he prayed, the conviction would rush upon him that all was true! —that all was true! and the prayer would be changed into cries of despair.

But a longing one evening came over him to go and gaze upon the house in which he knew Alice Lloyd to reside; and the desire at length overcoming his fears, he pulled his hat over his forehead, and enveloping himself in a cloak, walked rapidly forward, in the direction of Brompton.

They were evidently at home, for the drawing-room windows were illumined, and now and then he caught sight of a shadow moving across the

Venetian blinds, which were sufficiently open to render such a shadow visible.

He pressed his hand tightly across his heart, to subdue his emotion; and passing to the other side of the street, stood concealed in the shadow of a doorway, with his eyes fixed upon the houses opposite. It was a quiet neighbourhood, and but very few people were abroad. A policeman once or twice passed him, and glanced inquisitively at this cloaked figure standing so motionless, with its eyes fixed and staring from under the slouched hat, on the window over the way. But he might have thought it an assignation, the fair one not yet having made her appearance; and so turning the corner, he went shuffling along, gazing down into the kitchen windows, and envying the inmates, so cosily seated round the table or the fire, drinking tea and enlarging the housekeeping expenses.

Ah, Hamilton! hadst thou known the thoughts that choked the heart of that solitary watcher, so fixedly gazing upon the abode of his lost love, thou mightest have deemed, perhaps, the measure of thy revenge complete, and left thy victim to himself and to the fate which thou hadst woven round him!

He had not been standing there long before a brougham and two horses swept round the corner of the street, and pulled up in front of the house. He recognised the carriage at once as belonging to the Lloyds. The footman dismounted from the box, and rang the bell, and presently the door was opened by a servant. Seeing the carriage, she retired, evidently to inform those within the house that it was at the door.

The brougham was empty, and an idea that it might be destined to convey Alice either to a theatre or to a ball, suddenly took possession of Murray; a yearning to look upon her face again, perhaps for the last time, seized him; and, drawing his cloak yet more securely around him, he walked a little way down the street, and crossed over to the other side. Then advancing to the door belonging to the house next to the Lloyds', he posted himself in its shadow, and stood with a pale face and throbbing heart, looking on.

Suddenly the footman, who had been conversing with the coachman, turned his head, and, darting to the side of the carriage, opened the door, and lowered the steps. At the same moment, the sounds of a woman's voice laughing caused Murray to grasp the edge of the projecting doorway against which he was leaning, for support; and shortly after, Alice Lloyd, conducted by her father, passed from the house into the carriage. The rapid glance was sufficient to assure Murray that she was dressed for a ball, for the white satin had gleamed in the glare of the light, and he had noticed the flash of jewels upon her throat and on her arm.

" Now, papa, do go in," he heard her exclaim from the interior of the brougham; " you will catch cold out here; and, besides, you can hurry Frank, who is always such a time dressing."

Frank ! Murray remembered the name— Frank Collins ! Then he was going with her; alone ! If so, it was a sign of their engagement. Still grasping the edge of the wall, he stood motionlessly looking on.

" All right, my dear," said Mr. Lloyd, who was looking at his horses. " Now, take care of yourself; Good-night," and, waving his hand to her, he retired into the house. It was evident *he* was not going with her; and Murray knew well enough that Mrs. Lloyd never went out. It was certain then that she was going alone with Frank Collins to a party; and this was the tacit announcement of their engagement to be married.

A terrible desire to rush to the carriage and to strangle its inmate suddenly took possession of Murray. His fingers worked convulsively about; and he had need to exercise a mighty restraint upon his feelings to prevent himself from the perpetra· tion of some terrible deed. But the feeling after a few moments passed, and another desire equally strong set in—to speak to her, to tell her who he was, to stand before her and by his presence mar her evening's enjoyment :—for he could do no more.

Suddenly an opportunity presented itself. She put her head out of the window, and accosting the footman who stood by the side of the carriage, said,

"James, run in and ask Mary for my fan. I have left it on my bedroom table."

The footman disappeared, and on tiptoe Murray advanced to the brougham and looked in at her through the window.

The coachman had his chin on his breast and his eyes closed. The door of the house was also partially closed, perhaps by the footman, who with the habit peculiar to his species had mechanically pushed it to after him.

Alice's head was bent down, and she was

employed in buttoning a glove. As Murray's head came between her and the light from the street, she looked up, and seeing a stranger by her side, uttered an exclamation of alarm.

"You do not know me!" rapidly exclaimed Murray through his clenched teeth : "but *you* are familiar to me : *you* are Alice Lloyd—*I* am William Murray."

She did not utter a sound, but her face turned white as a corpse's, and she fixed her eyes upon his face with a dull, vacant stare.

"I have come to look at you for the last time!" he muttered in that deep whisper so ominously significant in a bad man's mouth; "I loved you once—you deserted me. I could have worshipped you—you have broken my heart. I curse you! Go to your dance and music, and forget William Murray if you can! Love others and forget his love if you can! Play with the world, and amidst your revelry forget *this*—the last gift of William Murray—if you can!"

He struck her a severe blow upon the mouth, and fled from the side of the carriage.

A long, wild shriek pealed from the lips of the poor girl, and the terrified coachman seeing the figure of Murray pass him, cut at him with his whip across the face and nearly blinded him—thinking him to be a thief who had attacked his mistress in the carriage. Mad with pain and rage, the cowardly wretch stooped down, and picking up a stone from the street, hurled it with all his strength at the coachman's head. It missed him, but struck the street lamp, and shivered the glass into a million splinters.

He waited to see no more. Gathering his cloak around him, he rushed down the street, turned the corner, and in a moment was out of sight.

The cry of alarm had brought everybody out of the house into the street; and all stood tremblingly around the carriage, inquiring the cause from the coachman, who could give them no information whatever. They found Alice in hysterics, crying and laughing by turns. They carried her up-stairs and put her to bed. A doctor was called and remedies applied, which after a while restored her sufficiently to enable her to communicate to her horrified listeners the scene that has been detailed. The vehemence of the ruffianly blow had been great enough to dislocate one of Alice's front teeth, and her upper lip was cut in a bad manner. In this sense he was right in his telling her to forget this, his last gift, if she could.

Early the next morning Mr. Lloyd lodged an action of assault against William Murray, and giving a Bow-street runner his description, offered him a handsome reward if he could find him out.

But Murray, anticipating such an event, took the precaution to change his clothes, his appearance, and his hotel; and, moreover, kept himself studiously concealed until the return of Belmont, which happened in less than a week after, when they both bade farewell to London and departed for Paris.

It may be needless to say that Murray never communicated the details of this scene to Belmont; thus keeping him in ignorance of a fact over which he might have exulted, as furnishing to his conscience one more plea to exonerate himself from his inward charge of remorselessness of revenge towards his foe, Mr. William Murray.

CHAPTER XI.

MISCARRIAGE.

It was a dark, tempestuous night. The wind howled through the streets of Paris with a violence that sometimes actually opposed the progress of those who, with bowed faces and coats tightly buttoned around them, endeavoured to stem its fury. Black and threatening clouds were chasing each other precipitately across the sky, and sometimes a heavy shower of rain that more resembled a broad sheet of water would be hurled against the roofs or the windows of the houses, instantly deluging the streets and flooding the gutters in a manner that rendered them impassable. Many of the streets were completely deserted; now and then a solitary vehicle would splash its way through the watery mud; but the night was so dark, the horses so frightened or jaded, and the gaslight from the side walks so flickering and uncertain, that the only aim of the drivers seemed to be to get home as soon as they could; in the soothing and cheering influence of a glass of sugar and water and a cigaret, to banish all thoughts of the misery from which they had so recently emerged. At least such would have been the conjecture of anyone willing to waste a few moments' reflection on these solitary vehicles as they passed him.

In the Rue Colville two lamps had been extinguished, and therefore only two remained to light the little street. But to judge from the utterly deserted appearance of the place, these two lights might also have been as well blown out; for the few and flickering rays they imparted were quite weak and useless. Many of the houses had their shutters tightly closed, perhaps fearful of the damage that the wind or rain promised to the unprotected glass; and this of course served to render the street more dark, as it now wanted what on a calmer evening it usually possessed—a little illumination from the interior of the rooms on the lower floors.

In No. 22, Rue Colville, in an apartment on the second story, two men were seated before a little fire, which one of them, a hunchback, would occasionally dive at with a poker that he held, either with a view of dissipating the *ennui* of silence, or of adding emphasis by gesticulation to the remarks he occasionally uttered.

"It's no use allowing yourself to be troubled with any compunctious visitings of remorse at the eleventh hour, you know, Williams; every thing's prepared, and—just hark at the wind!—what could be finer?"

"I wish I could feel remorse!" said Williams gloomily; "it is not conscience that restrains me now, it is something more degrading—fear."

"Of what?"

"Of detection."

"But who's going to detect us?"

"The ill-luck that has driven you and me to this act may yet pursue us with its frown, and mar the end—discovering us, and perhaps accommodating us at last with the irons of the galleys."

"Pish!" cried Sloman, lungeing at the fire, "if you commence the work with such forebodings as these—farewell to success; that's all I have to say. But it's all nonsense, man, these doubts. Look here! how are we to be detected? The thing is to be done noiselessly; an insertion of the key, an opening of the lid, an extraction of just enough to pave the way to——"

" Prison !"

" Fortune ! and then a silent exit with our pleasant wealth, which on the morrow may be restored with an ample apology for our previous want of ceremony."

Williams faintly smiled, and then relapsing into the frowning gravity that seemed now to have become habitual to him, he exclaimed, " All that you say is good for the morrow : but to-night has not yet passed."

" Well, it soon will, though.   By the way, what was the name of the man you took the impression to ?"

" Jacques Fourier, Rue St. Augustin."

" You were particular not to enter into much conversation with him ?"

" Why ?"

" Because if old Gautier should advertise our burglary, this Monsieur Jacques Fourier might be tempted to supply him or the police with the particulars that he is acquainted with."

" But what does he know ?"

" Enough to lead to detection.   Can't you understand, man ?   M. Jacques Fourier comes to M. Gautier, and says he, ' Monsieur, last Tuesday a young man entered my shop with an impression of a lock in wax, and requested me to make him a key for it. Here is the impression; apply it to your safe, and see if it fits.' "

" I understand."

" Of course old Gautier," continued Sloman, " would demand at once a description of the young man, and yours would be given."

" But I should never be suspected."

" Perhaps not by Gautier or his daughter—but you would by the police."

" Well ?"

" Well, if they should arrest you, *fear* might lead you into an avowal."

Williams bit his lips and gazed sternly at his companion. " You are right in thinking me a coward," he said, " for I confess I am one; but not exactly in the sense you mean. I fear detection, not for myself, but—but—"

" For what ?"

" Never mind; I am a little foolish, and—— what is the hour ?"

" About half-past nine."

" Two hours and a-half more."

" Yes. I hope the night will last as it is."

Williams arose and looked out of the window. " It is dark," he muttered to himself. " If I were superstitious, I might almost believe this to be a sign that we should succeed in our design." Then aloud he said, " It rains heavily."

" So much the worse for our skins," said Sloman.

" Everything will depend upon the strength of the fastening of the shutter. If it will not give to the lever, we shall not be able to enter."

" But it shall give !" cried Sloman. " Two fellows of our strength at the end of such an iron bar as that," he pointed to an instrument standing in the corner, " ought to be able to raise the house."

" Well, we shall see." And returning to his seat, the young man lighted a short pipe and commenced smoking in silence.

It was evident that their design to rob M. Gautier had been matured some time before; moreover, it is certain that they had fixed upon this particular night upon which to execute the robbery. For everything appeared prepared; a short crowbar had been purchased, and midnight was to be the hour of the attempt.

I do not think it necessary to pourtray to my reader, the emotions that agitated the heart of the young man pending the execution of his determination to commit the crime of robbery. The occasion that led him to it has been before sufficiently explained; and its reiteration, whilst it will not soften the wrong, can but fatigue the attention. For himself he saw but two things; the gaunt spectre of Famine driving him on behind to a Future, wreathed with smiles and bright in the light in which his imagination and his hopes enveloped it. To stop would be to perish; for he looked around him, and perceived nothing but want, despair, perhaps death. In his present position what was to be done? his pride prohibited him sinking to a lower grade for bread; and yet, strange contradiction! the pride that would have blushed at the bare thought of his occupying even for a short time a menial or a low position, rebelled not at that greater degradation which he was about to put upon himself; at that crime of which the committal was about to sink him to the level of the lowest grade of humanity, before whom the menials he despised were gentlemen — were nobility — were honest Men!

And yet let it not be thought that his scheme, hatched in an evil hour, was matured with all the coldness of a calculating scoundrel. Inherently his heart was noble — generous—fraught with those incipient virtues of which the full development means goodness and wisdom. But then he was young; and that word in the eyes of a philosopher, like Charity in those of the Divinity, covereth a multitude of sins. Had temptation alone been placed before him, he had spurned it with the indignant contempt of high resolve—of a generous disposition. But when it came allied to want—that gaunt spectre whose couched spear can put to flight the virtues of a world; when it came allied to Love—that syren whose smiles, when wrongfully given, serve but to illumine the way to despair; whose allurements can prompt the human mind to thoughts, and impel it to measures, such as the heart in its calm moments trembles to conceive, and dismisses as dreams too appalling to be remembered; when it came allied to his own desires—and to Sloman—we may condemn, yet we need not blush to own that our condemnation of the deed is tempered by our compassion for the doer.

His resolution once taken, necessity left him no room for hesitation. At the suggestion of Sloman, he had provided himself with a piece of wax, with which in a moment when M. Gautier slumbered upon the sofa, and Rosalie had left the room, he had pressed over the lock of the safe. He had also taken care to scrutinise the office which he and Sloman proposed forcing and entering. The shutters he had found to be closed (like most of the French shutters) with a hook on each side which, caught in a little staple, apparently not very strong. There was also a slight bar, that bolted the shutters together in the middle, but which, from its exceedingly rusty appearance, he concluded was seldom or never used. He knew not whether M. Gautier was in the habit of locking the office door at night; but he had not noticed a key in the lock.

The two men sat opposite each other for some time without speaking. Williams continued sucking the pipe in his mouth, his head slightly leaning back, and his eyes fixed on the wall over his companion. Sloman was growing sleepy; several times his chin bobbed against his breast, when he would jerk his head up again in a kind of amazement, his eyes wide open and staring around him. Then they would slowly reclose; his head would gradually sink until—pop! his chin would strike his breast, and up would jerk his head once more. This lasted until he fell asleep.

But there was no sleep for Williams. He almost envied that phlegmatic temperament of his companion which, with an enterprise before it involving hazard and perhaps great personal risk, could yet yield itself up to repose, and peacefully slumber.

He was greatly agitated. Indeed he did not dare contemplate the crime he had meditated. His mind was tumultuous with conflicting emotions, and many times his better feelings rose from out this confusion and almost inclined him to renounce his intention—to yield to the true impulse within him and to fly. But the shadow of his future, like night enveloping a world in darkness, stole over his soul and obscured those glimpses of pure light which had for a moment illumined him. Here almost in his grasp was the means to achieve, perhaps, the happiness of a life —and at what price? the stings of conscience which a confession and repentance would surely abate. But let him dash the opportunity down— fly from it like Joseph from the seductions of his tempter, and what would be the result? He could not tell—he saw only blackness before him, rayless, hopeless, comfortless: and it frightened him, and compelled him to turn back upon the opportunity which he had himself created—which was a crime, and his only hope!

He rose from his seat and went up-stairs to his room, and presently returned bearing in his hand a book. He seated himself and commenced to read. Page after page he turned over, and when he laid the volume down he found that he did not even know its name. Then he tried to imitate the example of his companion, who was now snoring, and composed himself to sleep. This lasted ten minutes; then he rose to his feet and going to the window, stood looking on to the blackness beyond. The rain had ceased, but the wind was still very violent, sweeping along the street and roaring down the chimney with the noise of thunder.

The time wore on, and suddenly he heard the tones of a distant clock rising and falling upon the boisterous night. He went over to the hunchback and shook him.

" Rouse up," he exclaimed; " it is twelve o'clock."

Sloman leapt to his feet, and rubbed his eyes.

" Twelve o'clock, is it? All right; where's the lantern ? "

Williams went to a cupboard, and produced a

small bull's-eye lamp. This he opened, and, applying a match to the wick, lighted it.

"You can carry it," said Sloman, "and I'll take the crow-bar. Wait until I put on my overcoat. Have you got on two pairs of socks?"

"Yes."

"All right. Here, take a pull at this," the hunchback said, holding out a brandy bottle to him; "drink some—it won't hurt you. A whole bottle of the stuff wouldn't hurt you in your present state of mind; you are too excited."

Williams turned a pale face to him, and said,—

"No; I am cool, collected. Look, this will show you how calm I am," and he held his hand out before Sloman; "you see it doesn't tremble."

"All right, my friend; we shall be back soon, a few pounds richer, I hope. Come on." He extinguished the light, and opening the lantern—which was a dark one—sufficiently to illumine their way down-stairs, he placed it in Williams' hand, and seized the iron bar. "Have you got the key?" he inquired, pausing on the threshold of the door.

"Everything."

"Lead the way, then," and with noiseless tread they went down-stairs, and got into the street.

The wind was so violent that they were compelled to grasp the masonry of the street-door for support. It blew so terribly, that they gazed up alarmed into the blackness above them, believing that the houses would be blown down, and they crushed beneath the *débris*. All at once, Sloman grasped his companion's arm.

"Hush!" he exclaimed, "do you hear?"

"What?"

"Here they come. Cower down, for fear they should see you," and the two men crouched beside the door.

At the same moment, Williams heard the clanking of sabres, and shortly after two mounted *gens-d'armes* passed by. When they were no longer audible, Sloman pointed to a lamp some little way down the street, and said,—

"That must be put out."

"I wish it were. But there's not much danger in it—see how it flickers; the light is too uncertain to be dangerous."

"Nevertheless, it must be put out. Come with me, and lend me a hand." They crossed the street, clinging to each other for fear of being blown down, and when they came to the lamp-post, Sloman said, "I have long arms, and can reach it better than you. Stoop your back, that I may get upon it."

Williams planted himself firmly against the lamp-post, and in an instant Sloman had leaped upon his shoulders and was climbing. A grotesque and extraordinary object he looked—like a huge toad, as he clung with his legs around the lamp-post, one hand grasping the projecting bar at the top, and the other employed in opening the window at the side. After much exertion, he succeeded in extinguishing the light; then, sliding down, he stood once more by the side of his companion.

"Wasn't that well done?" he exclaimed, with a hoarse chuckle.

"Admirable," said Williams.

"There isn't much fear about me, is there? Well, and now for business; come along," and, guiding themselves along the pavement, they approached the office window of M. Gautier's house.

"Unclose the light a little," whispered Sloman, "and direct it to the chink in the shutter; so —that will do. Not too much, man—not too much! It may be seen opposite."

The hunchback glanced cautiously around him, and listened. The wind howled down the street, accompanied now by a sharp rain that splashed in their faces and was slowly drenching them. Saving this war of the elements, no other sounds were audible, and after a little he raised the crowbar, and, inserting its sharp edge in the interstice caused by the fold of the shutters, he gave it a sudden and violent wrench. There was a noisy creak, but the shutters remained firm. Again he applied his strength to it, this time with a little more effect; the shutter partially opened, but on his relaxing his grasp, went back again to its place.

"Push a little with me," said Sloman.

Williams laid his hand upon the bar, and, at a signal from the hunchback, pushed whilst he pulled. The power was too great for the fastening; with a loud crack, which was drowned in the roar of the wind, the staple gave way, and the shutter flew open. Sloman pulled a piece of string from his pocket, and fastened the shutter securely to the wall by means of a short iron pin, which had been driven in there evidently for some such purpose.

"That will save it from banging about," he exclaimed; "and now for the window. But first listen."

The two men bent their heads and stood silent for a few moments. Then Sloman pointed to the window.

"We must crack that lower pane of glass," he whispered; "no, not you—let me do it. I fancy I know how it is done, without making much noise. How lucky it is that the wind is so high; we couldn't have done all this in a calm night."

Williams made no answer, but stood holding the lamp in such a position as to faintly illumine the glass.

Seizing the iron bar, Sloman struck the pane a smart blow, cracking it exactly in the centre. Then, turning to his companion, he asked him for his knife. Williams placed in his hands what he called a knife, but which in reality more resembled a dagger. The hunchback opened the blade, and, inserting it in one of the cracks, began to sway it to and fro. Presently he had loosened the piece of glass sufficiently to raise it high enough to place his finger beneath it; then, giving it a little tug, it came out, and he placed it carefully on the pavement. "The rest is easy," he exclaimed; and one after another he drew out the remaining portions of the window-pane, laying them each on the pavement, carefully and without any noise; then, collecting them together in a heap, he turned them over into the gutter.

"Now," he said, turning to Williams, and speaking hurriedly, "we have no time to lose. Get in, and go at once up-stairs—stay, though; there is the office-door to be opened yet. Try it; I will stop here. This shutter must be closed, else we may be discovered."

Williams crept in through the aperture, and at the same moment, Sloman, having unfastened the string, closed the shutter after him. The young man sat down and took off his boots, which he thrust into his side pockets, and, rising, advanced to the office-door and tried it. He found it unfastened, and, without pausing, glided noiselessly up-stairs. The door of the sitting-room was locked, but the key was in the lock. It grated harshly as he turned it, and he listened, fearing the noise might have disturbed the slumbering inmates of the rooms upstairs. He started, fancying he had heard a slight movement overhead, which he knew to be M. Gautier's room. But nothing but the howling of the wind was now audible, and, resolving to delay no longer, he pushed the door open and entered the apartment. The safe was in the corner where he had himself helped to place it some few evenings before ; and as the faint light from the lamp illumined the room, a momentary dizziness seized him, and he grasped the wall to support himself. For, after the safe, the next object his eyes had encountered was the sofa, and a sudden thought of Rosalie had swept across his mind, almost choking him with the emotions it had awakened in his heart. But clenching his teeth as if to subdue any thought likely to enervate him in this extraordinary moment, he approached the safe, and placing the lamp by his side, took a key out of his pocket and applied it to the lock.

The ponderous " click " of the latch had hardly ceased resounding through the room before a loud cry at the door caused him to look up with a terrified start, and he perceived the form of a man dressed in white levelling a pistol at his head. In an instant he had dashed the lamp over and extinguished it, and at the same moment the explosion of a cap announced that the trigger had been pulled, but that the pistol had missed fire.

" Thieves ! thieves ! " shrieked the man, whom Williams at once recognised by the voice to be

M. Gautier himself. " Help! murder!" and, dashing to a window, he hurled it open, and continued vociferating at the top of his voice, "Thieves! help! thieves! help!"

Darting out of the room, Williams glided like lightning down-stairs, and bursting open the shutter, passed through the aperture and gained the street. Sloman had vanished. Above him, he heard the voice of M. Gautier still screaming for assistance, and opposite, lights were flashing through the windows, some of which were open and peopled with heads and white faces. But something he heard seemed to smite upon his heart and cause him for a brief instant to totter. It was the clatter of horses in a gallop, accompanied by the cries of men and the clash of sabres.

Drawing his boots from his pocket, he thrust his feet hurriedly into them, and pulling his hat over his head, turned his face down the street, and rushed away at full speed.

CHAPTER XII.

ONCE MORE.

TAKING the streets as they came, without considering whither they were leading him, the young man pressed forward, panting, breathless, terrified, yet ever holding his rapid career, urged on by the imagined sounds of his pursuers behind.

Not a human being was visible. Paris on that particular night seemed like a huge necropolis, but for the ruddy light streaming through the occasional windows, indicating the presence of life and animation.

Exhausted by the violence of his flight, he at last slackened his speed, and finally stopped and leant against the interior of a doorway to recover his breath.

He strained his attention to hear, if he could, the sounds of those dreaded pursuers, the *gens-d'armes*, who, he knew, were scouring the neigh-

Q 2

bourhood of the Rue Colville to find him. Suddenly he heard the clattering of footsteps coming down a street near him, and presently the figure of a man running turned the corner with extraordinary rapidity, and flew past him. A murmur of astonishment escaped the panting lips of the young man, and he cried at the top of his voice, "Sloman!"

The figure stopped with a sudden jerk, and turned round.

"Sloman!" repeated Williams, emerging from his dark recess, and walking towards the hunchback.

Sloman raised his arms in the air with astonishment.

"Well, this is singular, too! funny meeting you here!"

In spite of the rapidity of his pace, which he must have held for some considerable time, this extraordinary being seemed not in the least degree distressed. He did not even pant, but, grasping Williams by the arm, exclaimed,—

"Come on; it won't do for us to stand talking here. We can discuss the matter as we walk."

"Where shall we go to?"

"Anywhere; but far from here, at all events."

"I have not a penny in my pocket; we shall therefore have to walk all night."

"I think not," answered the hunchback, coolly. "There are a few francs in my pocket—enough to provide us with a bed."

"Thank Heaven!" murmured the young man. "I am cold—weary. I should die before morning in the streets."

"What on earth gave the old miser the alarm? He cried out loud enough to waken the whole city."

"I moved softly," said the young man; "I made no noise—it must have been Providence."

A profane remark was Sloman's reply, and he added,—

"If I had had the managing of it, all would have gone well."

"Well!" cried Williams, bitterly; "ah, crime never succeeds in this world."

"Pish, man! it was our ill luck. Had the old brute slept only a few minutes longer, all would have gone exactly as we wished. I suppose the wind kept him awake and made him nervous, and you must have made some noise which brought him down."

"That may be; at any rate, I have had a

narrow escape of my life. He aimed a pistol at me that missed fire—there was no ill-luck there. Ah, 'twas a narrow escape!" and Williams shuddered violently. Then he murmured, "It is cold —bitterly cold."

"We must walk yet," said Sloman. "We are outcasts now. We can never return to the Rue Colville."

Williams made no reply, but with chattering teeth and clenched hands walked rapidly on by the side of his almost trotting companion.

"The *gens-d'armes* will be upon our track as safe as possible," continued Sloman. "The moment our landlord finds we are missing, he will lay information against us. He knows us so well, too! What are we to do? All my money is at my rooms—all my clothes. I shall be a beggar unless I regain them."

"All your money!" exclaimed Williams, turning his pale face to his companion, with a look of astonishment.

"Yes—that is to say, the very little I managed to save," muttered Sloman, in an embarrassed manner.

"I thought you were a beggar."

"So I am."

"Now; but if you had money you were not."

Sloman made no reply, but moved forward with still greater rapidity.

"It was under the supposition that you were penniless," continued Williams, violently panting, "that I prevailed upon myself to undertake this affair. Why did you not tell me you had money? It would have saved us both from this."

"I cannot enter into any explanations now," replied the hunchback, doggedly. "I am too tired. To-morrow—any time—not now. You are right—it is terribly cold, and I am wet through to the skin. How high the wind is."

Williams bit his lip to stifle the angry syllables that had else escaped him; and now, too exhausted to converse, the two men continued their rapid flight in silence.

They were approaching the outskirts of the City, and had placed in streets some three or four miles between them and the scene of their late adventure. The houses were now rapidly thinning, and stood in small groups, or detached, on either side the road they were pursuing. The night still continued tempestuous; but the clouds above had broken, and through their jagged edges could be caught occasional glimpses of the black sky, studded with stars. Suddenly Williams halted.

"I can go no further," he exclaimed; "leave me here, and go you on. I would die now, for there is nothing to live for."

"Nonsense," answered Sloman, who appeared as fresh as at the moment of starting, and whose short bow-legs travelled over the ground with unwearying rapidity; "I know where we are, and I also know that there is an hotel somewhere in the neighbourhood. It is a little further on, and there we can get a night's shelter. To-morrow we must be up, and see about the Rue Colville — whether there is any danger in our returning, and so forth. Perhaps, after all, our fear may be imaginary. How are they to know that we were the robbers? We can invent a thousand excuses to account for our absence from our rooms; and unless old Gautier spied you, I don't see how we are to be accused. In fact, I really don't know what made us bolt away so hard. We might have stood at our door, and pretended we had been alarmed by the miser's outcry. Ah, it strikes me we have been playing the fool."

"Fools or not, I am dying!" panted the

young man; "lead me to a bed, or leave me here to die—I can go no further."

Sloman glanced around him, and seemed to reflect; then he exclaimed,—

"Come on a little way yet. I know there is an hotel somewhere about here, called 'La Maison Rouge.' I remember having read the advertisement. As to dying, that is all nonsense. Men don't die so easily. To-morrow you will be well, and then we shall try and find our way back to our lodgings. And as to old Gautier, we'll rob him yet—if only to spite the noisy scoundrel!"

And he struck his clenched fist in his hand, and swore a great oath.

The character of the hunchback was certainly a paradox. Here he was—cold, wet, his hopes blasted, beggary staring him in the face, the law perhaps at his back, and, worst of all, his money, which he had so sedulously concealed from Williams, for aught he could tell, irretrievably lost—I say, yet here he was, conversing in a tone that seemed almost cheerful; his irritability being alone discernible in the occasional blasphemy with which he interlarded his phrases.

Was this the result of any fresh scheme

which his busy brain was now shadowing forth, and of which he destined his young companion to be the instrument or the medium of its operations? I know not. But whether or not, his machinations were doomed to meet with a sudden and unexpected conclusion.

Grasping his companion by the arm, Williams proceeded wearily to move forward again, the hunchback meanwhile gazing anxiously around him. All at once he uttered a cry.

"There is the hotel," he exclaimed. "I knew I was right. Don't you see that dark house standing alone there at the corner?"

"Yes."

"Well, there we shall be able to get a bed, and I daresay a glass of hot brandy and water."

They now approached the house, and in the dim light given forth from the rifts in the clouds, Williams perceived a sign-board suspended over the door, though what was written on it he could not perceive.

"Will they let us in?" he asked.

"Why shouldn't they?"

"But it is one o'clock."

"Not yet. But if it were, what then? I suppose they keep open all night. At all events if knocking will open the door we'll be let in," and he made a movement as if to step forward.

"Stop," exclaimed Williams, grasping him by the arm, "will not our appearance excite suspicion? Just look at me! I am spattered with mud; and know I look pale as a ghost."

Sloman reflected for a few moments, and then said,—

"Leave everything to me. I'll give 'em a story to account for our looks. Only mind you say yes to everything I may propose."

The hunchback inspected him in silence for a little while, and then said,—

"All right; your appearance will assist my invention. Now come along."

And they proceeded up to the door of the hotel, which was closed, and rang long and heavily.

They could now read the sign-board, and Sloman said,—

"You see I was right; it is 'La Maison Rouge' as I thought."

In reality the house was less an hotel than an inn: it being one of those buildings more frequently met with in the environs of Paris than in Paris itself, which assume all the dignity of the

hotel without the proportions or dimensions sufficient to vindicate the assumption.

After a little, a noise was heard approaching
them from the interior, and presently the door
was cautiously opened, and the head of a *garçon*
popped out.

" *Qui est là ?* " said he.

" Open the door. We are travellers. We seek
accommodation for the night," replied Sloman,
in tolerable French.

"What country are you ?" inquired the *garçon*,
still holding his cautious position, and eyeing the
two men inquisitively.

Without replying, Sloman pushed the door
open, squeezing the waiter behind it, and shouted
to Williams to follow him.

When inside, the hunchback turned to the
garçon, who was gazing upon him with an
alarmed countenance, and demanded to see the
landlord.

" He is in bed, Monsieur," said the *garçon*.

" Who are you, then ? "

" I am the night-porter."

" Very well. We are two young Englishmen
who, on our way from ——, have been overtaken
and robbed. We have had a hard run for our

lives, and that accounts for our appearance. We want a fire, some brandy and water, and a bed. We can pay for it."

And Sloman significantly smote his pockets, making some coins concealed therein utter an expressive, and perhaps, to the *garçon*, a soothing sound. For the doubtful look upon his face relaxed, and making a short bow to the hunchback, he said,—

"You are late, gentlemen. It is just upon one o'clock. Nevertheless, there is a little fire still burning in the coffee-room, where you can repose yourselves until your beds are ready. Will you have two rooms?"

"What are your charges?"

"We have rooms varying from five francs to thirty sous per night."

"Prepare for us two thirty-sous rooms. But. lead us meanwhile to your coffee-room; we are wet and cold, and need warmth. Look at my comrade; he is quite exhausted."

The *garçon* bent a sympathetic eye upon Williams, whose appearance indicated a degree of suffering sufficient to have awakened pity in the heart of a misanthrope, and then turning to Sloman asked him to follow him.

He led them down a passage; and through a

glass window, let in perhaps for the convenience of the waiters, who could thus perceive the movements of the inmates, Sloman saw a little fire cheerily burning in a grate.

"Is that the coffee-room?" he asked.

"Yes, Monsieur; this way, please." And opening a side door, he bade them enter.

Williams walked directly up to the fire, and seizing an arm-chair, flung himself into it in the very last stage of weariness. Sloman took a seat opposite.

"Will you not have something to eat?" asked the *garçon*.

Sloman glanced at Williams, who shook his head.

"No, we want nothing to eat. Merely get us some hot brandy and water at once."

The *garçon* left the room, and the two men found themselves alone.

"Do you think he believed our story?" asked Sloman.

Williams gave a faint shrug of the shoulders.

"A little repose!" he murmured; "I am faint and weak. I can hardly speak."

The hunchback glanced at him with compassion. The sufferings, mental and physical, of the young man, had actually touched the heart of this strange creature.

"You had better go to bed at once," he said. "You are ill. First have the brandy, and then off with you. A warm blanket will put you to rights: and to-morrow you will find yourself well."

The young man shook his head with a gesture full of despair. Interpreted aright, it told of remorse, of suffering, perhaps of death.

The *garçon* soon made his appearance, bearing two tumblers steaming with their grateful contents. Williams seized the glass held out to him, with a trembling hand, and raised it to his lips.

At that moment a violent ringing of the bell caused the waiter to give a great start; then turning abruptly on his heel he left the room.

A post-chaise with two horses was standing in front of the house, and in it were seated three figures, one of which, when the door was opened, cried out,—

"Can you give us a bed here?"

"Yes, Monsieur!" answered the *garçon*.

The man that had spoken held a short consultation with the figure seated by his side, and then dismounting approached the *garçon*.

"How far are we from Paris?" he asked.

"You are in Paris now, Monsieur."

"Yes: I mean what is the distance from here to the Boulevards —— ?"

"About a league and a quarter."

"What sort of accommodation have you here?"

"Very good, Monsieur."

"Can you provide us with something to eat?"

"You can have what you like."

The man went back to the post-chaise.

"We had better stay for to-night," he said. "My clothes are damp, and perhaps we may not get admission into the Hotel de la Grande Bretagne."

"As you will," responded the person accosted. And rising, he descended to the ground, and stood by the side of his companion.

"What is your charge?" said the first speaker, addressing the remaining figure in the vehicle.

"Three napoleons, sir."

The man put his hand in his pocket and produced the money, which he held out.

"Do you intend returning to D—— to-night?" he inquired.

"No, sir. There's a hostelry not far from here where I shall put up. Here are your portmanteaus." The speaker handed some luggage out of the bottom of the chaise, and then saying, "*Bon soir, Messieurs*," flipped the horses, and drove off.

The two men, grasping their luggage, entered the hotel.

"Are you the only person up?" inquired one of them of the *garçon*.

"Belonging to the hotel, Monsieur. But I can call up Maitre Fordiat, the landlord, if Monsieur will."

"There is no occasion for it. This villanous night has nearly been the death of us. The diligence from S—— where the train stopped (what trains you have in this country!) overturned halfway between S—— and here. A miserable auberge at D—— could afford us no accommodation except the chaise that you saw us come in, and so we've been obliged to post it through this conflict of the elements. Show us to a room."

"Would Monsieur like a private room?"

"Anywhere with a fire."

"There is a fire in the coffee-room."

"That will do."

The *garçon* conducted them as he had conducted his former visitors, down the passage; but as they passed the window one of the two uttered a cry, and grasped his companion's arm.

"Look!" he hoarsely exclaimed, pointing to the figure of the hunchback, whose outline was strongly marked against the ruddy background of the fire. "Is it a ghost—a phantom? Look!"

The man addressed turned his eyes in the direction indicated by the pointing finger of his companion; and then in a low, suppressed voice, muttered,—

"It is Sloman!"

There was a moment's pause, and the two continued speechless, gazing at the figure of the hunchback. Suddenly one of them made a step forward.

"Where are you going to?" whispered his friend, detaining him by the arm.

"To strangle him!" was the hoarse reply. "Let me go, Belmont; he shall not escape me."

"You are mad. This will be murder, and you will be hanged!"

"There will be murder in this house before morning!" and the speaker stamped his foot as he continued glaring at the hunchback.

"Will you follow me, gentlemen?" said the *garçon*, who had been silently standing by.

"Show us to a private room," said Belmont; "and—Murray," he continued, his grasp of his companion's arm still unrelaxed, "be guided by me. You must not be rash—murder is not your game!"

A low, bitter growl was Murray's only reply. The sight of the hunchback seemed to have made him frantic.

"Now, lead the way to a private room—at once!" said Belmont imperiously to the *garçon*. Then aside to Murray, he whispered, "We do not want them to see us here."

Murray, passive in the powerful grasp of his companion, suffered himself to be led up-stairs; and the waiter conducted them into a private room. He then supplied them with lights, and applied a match to a prepared fire in the grate.

"What orders, gentlemen?" he asked.

"Something to eat," answered Belmont; "and some hot water and brandy."

The *garçon* went away; and throwing his coat and hat upon a chair, Murray commenced violently to pace the room.

Belmont eyed him in silence a little, and then said,—

"After this let no man have any doubt in

chance. Was there ever anything more marvellous than this meeting?"

"But whilst you are talking," Murray exclaimed, excitedly, waving his hands to and fro, and speaking through lips pale with passion, "he may escape us. Let him have but an inkling of our presence, and he will fly!"

"Nonsense, man! he is booked here for the night; couldn't you see that?"

"It is your conjecture," muttered Murray, resuming his violent pacing. "If we lose him we may meet him no more."

"And if you should go down to him now, what would you do?" and Belmont, as he put the question, fixed his eyes full on those of his companion.

"Do!" Murray paused; then approaching Belmont close, he half hissed, "I would seize him by the throat, and demand my money back, and those documents he robbed me of. If he would not surrender them, I would strangle him where he stood, and fling his body into the street, proclaim myself his murderer, and let the law do its worst!"

In his excitement he had stretched forth his arm as if he meant to put his menace against

Sloman into execution upon Belmont. His companion coldly returned the fierce gaze that was fastened upon him.

"Do you understand now what I would do to him?" said Murray, with a terrible smile.

"Perfectly. And that is what you call revenge?"

"Would it not be?"

Belmont shrugged his shoulders.

"That is one kind of revenge; but there are other modes of avenging one's wrongs."

Murray made no answer, but folded his arms tightly over his breast, and recommenced his pacing.

A light smile flitted across Belmont's face.

"I wonder," he said, "who his companion is?"

"Some villain—be sure of that!"

"Come, sit down, and have patience. First eat your supper and drink some spirits. Then go to bed and renew your strength by sleep, to enable you to achieve successfully whatever you may undertake."

Murray came moodily to a chair and seated himself.

"I have a pistol in my travelling bag," Belmont said, carelessly. "I always find them useful. But then they are rather cumbersome to carry about; and so I prefer this sort of thing." As he spoke he slipped his hand into his bosom, and drew out a small sheathed dagger.

Murray's eyes flashed as he gazed at it, and he exclaimed,—

"I wish I had provided myself with one of those. Let me see it."

Belmont handed it over to him. Murray examined it in silence, then laid it by his side upon the table. At this moment the waiter entered bearing a tray. Whilst laying the cloth, Belmont said to him,—

"Have you not two gentlemen below in the coffee-room?"

"They have just gone to bed, sir."

"Oh; do you know anything of them?"

"Nothing, sir, beyond that they came to this house about three quarters of an hour ago or so, saying they had been robbed, and had to run for their lives."

"Humph!"

"The young man with the gentleman with the hump appeared terribly fatigued. I felt rather suspicious, but as they had money I could not refuse them admittance. Monsieur will pardon me," continued the *garçon*, turning with a smile to Belmont, "but——"

"What?"

"Have I Monsieur's permission for what I am going to say?"

The *garçon* was smiling with a dubious expression, and Belmont eyed him with surprise.

"But what is it, man?"

"Well, Monsieur, if you will pardon me, I must say that in all my life I never saw such a resemblance between two strangers as there is between you and the young man who was in the coffee-room when you entered. A thousand pardons for the liberty, but I could swear that Monsieur was the young man's father."

Belmont laughed, and shrugged up his shoulders.

"I am often mistaken for other people," said he drily to Murray; "that is one of the misfortunes of my face."

Murray glanced at him, and answered,—

"To tell you the truth, at certain times you occasionally remind me of some one I was acquainted with, years ago."

"Ha! ha! now isn't that singular! What was your friend's name?"

"Oh, nobody you know. It was—it was—let me see. Hamilton—ah, Hamilton!"

"That is curious. But all things are possible in this world, Murray. Come, the supper is ready. Let us enjoy life whilst we have it." And apparently in a cheerful humour, Belmont drew near the table, and commenced carving a cold fowl.

As the *garçon* was leaving the room, Murray rose and went after him. At the door he asked him something in a whisper; and after a few moments' hesitation the man replied in the same low voice. Then Murray returned to the table and took his seat in silence. Once when Belmont was looking another way he slipped the dagger upon the table into his pocket.

Half an hour passed away, and two o'clock struck. Murray stood up and held his hand out to Belmont. "I am going to bed," he said. "I am sleepy. Good-night."

"Good-night; and a pleasant repose to you, after the hardships, first of all, of a French train, then a French diligence, and finally a French post-chaise."

Murray did not smile, but after a little hesitation, he said in an agitated manner, "Mr. Belmont, you have been a good friend to me, and from my heart I thank you for your kindness. Should anything ever happen to me, be sure that I left you at least with grateful feelings."

A hard, almost malignant, smile gathered around Belmont's lips, and he answered: "Whatever I have done for you has been done willingly. Believe that, and I shall consider myself amply rewarded. To-morrow we will be up before Sloman, follow his movements, and pursue him to his lair. Once trapped, the fellow will be at our mercy."

"Well, good-night," was all Murray's reply; and snatching up a candle he left the room.

Ten minutes after this Belmont took a candle and went up-stairs. He glanced at Murray's bedroom door as he passed, and observed it was closed.

The next moment he had entered his own apartment and closed the door.

*   *   *   *
*   *   *   *

He was awakened the next morning by a loud rapping. Leaping out of bed, he slipped on his clothes and hastened to inquire what was the matter. He encountered the *garçon* of the preceding evening standing on the threshold of the apartment, his face white, his eyes dilated, his whole aspect denoting the intensest horror.

"Oh, Monsieur!" he cried the moment he caught sight of Belmont.

"What is it?" demanded Belmont.

"Oh, Monsieur, your friend, the hunchback—both! *mais, c'est effrayant!*"

Belmont grasped him by the arm, and with a frown of impatience bade him speak out.

"They are dead, sir," gasped the man. "Both killed!"

"Conduct me to their room—quick!" and following the waiter Belmont hastily ascended the stairs.

Around the door of an apartment situated on the last story but one, a group of persons was assembled speaking in whispers, with blanched cheeks and trembling lips. Their eyes were bent upon some object on the floor, and ever and anon an ejaculation of horror would escape one of them, and the murmur would be taken up by the whole group. Then would fall a dead stillness, then again the whispering would go on.

Forcing his way through these people, who comprised the whole establishment of the "Maison

Rouge," Belmont passed into the apartment, and gained the side of the proprietor of the hotel, who stood looking on with hair erect and open mouth.

It was a fearful sight!

They must have had a long struggle; for they were both locked in each other's embrace. Sloman was the under man. There was a black pool stagnating around them, and on each face rage and agony had stamped their expression.

The posture of Sloman was hideously grotesque. Being on his back, his hump had thrown up his body and his head had fallen back, his fixed eyes keeping a dead, inverted gaze upon the group around the door; his two legs were coiled around Murray's in the most extraordinary manner, and apparently with a view of breaking the limbs of his adversary, who was clutched in his amazing hold with the power of a vice.

And the mysterious fatality that had dogged these two men since the commission of their first, blackest crime seemed to have reached its climax in this: that the weapons with which this double murder had been perpetrated were supplied by those whom the dead men in life had most bitterly wronged.

The knife that Sloman had employed was the one given to him by Williams to separate the pieces of glass from M. Gautier's broken window. That used by Murray was the weapon taken by him a few hours before from Belmont.

So the son, no less than the father, had contributed to the destruction of these men—the murderers of Eveleen, the wife, and the mother: the outragers of Hamilton, the husband, the father, and the man!

The deadly conflict must have been waged silently; for none in the house had been disturbed. And it was the more horrible to reflect upon it thus: for those who gazed upon these two lifeless bodies well knew the deadliness of the impulse that had urged them, and held them dumb amidst their dark deed.

With folded arms Belmont stood surveying this group upon the floor. His face was pale and his lips were tightly compressed; but with these exceptions, no other signs in his appearance testified to the effect of this spectacle upon his feelings.

To have watched him as he stood thus, you would have thought that he had anticipated this result; had expected some such conclusion in the drama of which he was a chief actor; and because of his having so long foreseen the end, now that it was come, it caused in him no surprise, no other emotions than such as could not fail to be provoked by the real, terrible, embodiment of his old meditations.

CHAPTER XIII.

FATHER AND SON.

"Sir," said the proprietor of "La Maison Rouge," his face white with horror, and pointing to the floor, "do you know anything of this?"

"Nothing more than what I see," said Belmont. "By the way, hadn't that hunchback a friend here with him last night?"

"Yes, sir," said the *garçon*, who formed one of the group at the door.

"Where is he?"

"He still sleeps, sir."

"You had better go and rouse him."

The *garçon* was some time absent; when he returned, the proprietor said, "*Eh bien, Jacques,* is he coming?"

"Yes, sir. The poor man seemed very weary, and I had some difficulty in waking him up."

"Perhaps he can shed some light on this mystery, sir," remarked the proprietor to Belmont.

Belmont shrugged his shoulders. "It is a horrible affair."

"Horrible indeed," ejaculated the proprietor. Then raising his voice, he said to one of the men at the door, "Augustin, go and fetch M. Malherbe; tell him what has occurred, and ask him to come at once."

"Who is M. Malherbe?" asked Belmont.

"The commissary of the police," said the proprietor.

"Ah. I hope this dreadful occurrence won't injure the reputation of your house."

The proprietor cast his eyes devoutly up to the ceiling and exclaimed, "We are all in the hands of Providence, Monsieur."

"You are right," said Belmont. Then fixing his eyes upon the dead bodies he remained lost in thought.

Presently there was a movement at the door, and somebody cried, "This way, sir." The group divided itself and made a passage for Williams, who entered the room in a nervous and agitated manner. No sooner did he catch sight of the bodies, than he stopped as if transfixed, his hands spread out before him, his eyes dilated, and his mouth a little open. Then he looked around him with a bewildered and terrified stare. "What does that mean?" he asked, pointing to the floor.

At the first sound of his voice, Belmont started, and laid his hand upon his heart to subdue the sudden throbbing that the tones seemed to have provoked. There was also a little murmur amongst the group at the door, and a voice said in a whisper,—

"Are not their voices wonderfully alike?"

"We do not know," answered the proprietor, "and we have taken the liberty of calling you in, in order to ascertain whether you know anything about this horrible mystery."

The young man had hidden his face in his hands, and was shaking his head. The spectacle seemed to overpower him, and he strove to blot it from his sight.

Belmont's eyes were fixed upon him with a strange, earnest, penetrating stare. That mysterious influence which the presence of the parent exercises over the child—the child over the parent —was upon him; a wild, a nameless exultation at the first accents of his son's voice, had thrilled the soul of the father: and again he pressed his hand upon his breast to still the sudden beating that came like a succession of shocks from his heart, and which promised to overpower him, unless subdued at once. The very attitude that the young man had assumed was his. The bowed head, the hands clasped over the face, the motionless posture, and the attitude so dignified, and yet so full of repose, were Hamilton's. He recognised them as his; and a strange voice was in his heart whispering to him that he had at length found his son.   .

But he dreaded the vainness of this intuitive conjecture—this inward conviction which was yet unratified by inquiry; and he longed for the moment when he might draw the young man aside by himself and question him alone.

Suddenly a bustle was heard on the stairs, and amidst a murmur of respect the Commissary, M. Malherbe, entered, important in a cocked hat, which he took off as he saluted the company. He frowned as he fixed his gaze on the bodies, and exclaimed,—

"They are dead!"

"And cold," answered the proprietor of "La Maison Rouge."

"Ma foi!" said M. Malherbe, stroking his moustache; "but they must have had a terrible

conflict. Look at the expressions of their faces."
And going up to the dead men he touched
Sloman's arm. "What is known of this?"
he suddenly exclaimed, throwing a frowning
glance around him.

The proprietor briefly informed him that the
discovery that they were dead was all that had as
yet been ascertained. Then pointing to Belmont
and Williams he told him those gentlemen were
friends of the deceased.

The pale face of Williams attracted the attention of M. Malherbe.

"Relate," he said, in an imperious manner,
"what you know of your friend. Which of the
two was it?"

"*Le Bossu!*" exclaimed Jacques, from the
door.

"What did, or do you know, of the hunchback?" said M. Malherbe.

Williams eyed him with a disdainful look, and
answered coldly,—

"My first acquaintance with him was at the
Café Victoire, Rue ——"

"Oh! Is that all you know of him?"

"I also lodged in the same house he occupied
in the Rue Colville."

"Ah! the street of last night's robbery?"

"Was there a robbery there, sir?" asked the proprietor, who, having supped plentifully of horrors, was yet eager for more.

"Yes," said M. Malherbe, who loved to enumerate his knowledge of human crime, fancying that it added something to his importance; "at the house of one M. Gautier, money-lender."

"Have the thieves been discovered?"

"One has been apprehended, but he escaped."

"Escaped!"

"Yes," said M. Malherbe, shrugging his shoulders, "through the clumsiness of Maitre Loquert, who will certainly be discharged. The idiot, instead of handcuffing him, seized him by the arm, fancying himself a match for the scoundrel; but he was overturned in the gutter, with a severe bruise upon the head, and the man escaped in the darkness. However, he will be sure to be caught, as it is supposed there is only one of them. At least, so M. Gautier said."

"And was any money stolen?" asked the inquisitive proprietor.

Fortunately for his curiosity he was possessed of a good cellar, otherwise it may be doubted whether M. Malherbe would have gratified him by so many replies.

"I haven't heard, for the old money-lender it appears died before he could conclude his evidence. The fright killed him."

It was certainly lucky for Williams that M. Malherbe had his head turned another way, else the mortal paleness that suddenly overspread the young man's countenance would infallibly have led to his conviction. Belmont noticed his agitation, and believing him to be ill, sprung forward and pushed a chair beneath him, into which he sank.

"This young gentleman is very unwell," said Belmont to M. Malherbe, who had turned his face once more to resume his examination. "I believe I can furnish you with more evidence connected with this horrible affair than he. Look, I will give you my address; apply to us both there when you wish to examine us for the inquest." And extracting a card, he wrote upon it, "Hôtel de la Grande Bretagne," and handed it to the Commissary.

The manner and the language of Belmont sufficiently denoted his superiority; and with the politeness of a Frenchman, M. Malherbe bowed, and placed the card in his pocket.

"I cannot of course detain you," he said; "messieurs, you are at liberty to depart when you like." Then he added to himself, "But I will place them both under *surveillance*."

"Come," said Belmont, laying his hand upon Williams' shoulder, "let us leave this room of death. We will have more air down-stairs, and," he added, in a low voice, "we shall be free from the annoyance of this fellow's questioning."

The young man rose, and mechanically followed his new friend. The group at the door made way for them to pass, and whispered,—

"Oh Ciel! what an extraordinary resemblance."

Belmont led the way into the private apartment which he had occupied the preceding evening, and touching the bell, requested the young man to be seated. A *garçon* who had followed them knocked at the door and demanded to know what they wanted.

"Procure us some breakfast," said Belmont, "and get me my bill."

"Shall I bring yours too, monsieur?" asked the *garçon*, looking at Williams.

He blushed, and hesitated. His hands instinctively sought his pockets, and then clasped themselves with a gesture of despair upon his knee. Belmont comprehended at a glance that his companion was without money, and turning to the waiter, he exclaimed,—

"Yes; bring this gentleman's bill too."

As the door closed, Williams raised his eyes to Belmont's face, and in a voice broken with emotion, said,—

" Sir, you have told this man to bring me my bill. It will be useless, as I cannot pay it. I am a beggar. The dead man up-stairs, whose name was Sloman, had a few francs in his pocket, and to him I looked for the discharge of this debt."

"It does not matter," said Belmont; "I shall be most happy to lend you the necessary sum. You can repay me at your convenience."

Williams coloured up, and remained for a short while silent; then glancing at Mr. Belmont, he said,—

" I have been so little accustomed to kindness, that I can find no language to express my feelings to you. But," he added, bitterly, "if you knew me as I know myself, you would spurn me from you, and think yourself contaminated by having been in my presence. Ay, death alone

can expiate this injury! and she—and she——"
he paused, and buried his face in his hands, moving his body to and fro with the vehemence of
the grief that consumed him.

Belmont eyed him a short while in silence, and
then tenderly inquired the cause of his sorrow.

"I am a murderer!" cried the young man,
leaping to his feet, and heavily striking his breast
with his clenched fist. "A murderer—ay! the
murderer of my earliest friend—the murderer of
my darling's father!"

A dark look of anxiety swept across the features of Belmont.

"Tell me," he exclaimed, in a tremulous voice,
"why do you accuse yourself of murder?"

"Why? Oh, this crowning misery! Was
there no better fate in store for me than that
I should be subjected to the temptation of this
cruel wrong. And she—she will curse me—hate
me—spurn me from her as his murderer, and I
shall be dumb before her!"

"I wish to be your friend," said Belmont.
"Gratify my wish by communicating to me the
cause of your suffering. If you have committed
a murder—then Heaven help you!"

The young man pushed his chair close to him,

and seated himself in it. Then seizing Belmont's arm, he murmured in a low tone,—

"You have made yourself my friend now, only to loathe me with more bitterness when you shall have heard my story. But it matters not. Hate, love, these words exist no longer for me. I have been long in the world alone, and I shall leave it desolately as I entered it."

He pressed his hand over his forehead for a few moments as if striving to collect his thoughts, and relaxing his hold of his companion's arm, he fixed his eyes upon the ground, and in a low voice commenced the narrative of the last few months, from his first introduction to Mr. Brown, to the present moment. He omitted nothing. As if the disclosure relieved him, like the hot tears that occasionally dimmed his eyes, he poured forth his story, his companion the while listening to him with gaze riveted upon his bowed face. All the circumstances of his first meeting with Sloman, his poverty that compelled him to the gambling-house, his ill-luck that in- cited him to the crime causing the death of old Gautier, he minutely revealed. The influence exerted over him by the presence of Belmont— a presence rendered so sweet by the sympathy it expressed, awakened his heart into a full disclosure of its most hidden thoughts—thoughts that he had even fancied were concealed from himself, and which, as they trembled from his lips, thrilled him with the strange and new emotions they imparted.

At length he ceased, and timidly raised his eyes to his companion's face. Belmont wore a grave, anxious, almost dubious expression. He seemed unsatisfied. Something was wanting, and that something had not yet been communicated.

"And where," he asked, "did you first make the acquaintance of M. Gautier?"

"At a small town called Fernley."

"Is that near Henley-on-Thames?"

"About fifteen miles or so."

"Do you know Henley?"

The anxious look on Belmont's face grew keen, and he bent his head forward to catch the reply.

"I was born there," said Williams.

The father choked the sudden cry that had almost burst from his lips, and his whole form trembled with a violence that alarmed his companion.

"You are not well," he exclaimed.

"Yes—yes—a spasm—a pain—no more. Tell

me, what do you recollect of Henley? Do you remember—your—mother?"

The question seemed to cause him a sudden agony, for he pressed his hand to his heart as he spoke.

"No; I never saw her. I do not even know her name. I had an aunt called Miss Godstone, who sometimes mentioned her by the name of Eveleen; but I was very young. I can remember little except cruel treatment——"

He suddenly paused, and rose with a movement of alarm.

Belmont had risen to his feet, and stood with clasped hands looking up to heaven. His lips were moving as if in prayer, and his face wore an expression of grandeur that made the young man look at him with awe—almost terror.

He continued gazing upwards with a look of sublime devotion; then, dashing the heavy drops from his eyes, the father sprang to the side of his son, and clasped him to his heart.

"I am your father," he cried. "I am he who knew not of your existence; who has yearned for you day and night with a heart broken by the wrongs of remorseless enemies—with a heart broken by the separation from her to whom you owe your existence! Look up at me! Bless me with the sight of those eyes that my darling in heaven saw not! Oh, Eveleen! seest thou now the happiness of thy husband and thy son? Speak to me, my child; look up——"

He suddenly stopped, and with a hurried and trembling hand raised the face of his child that was bowed upon his breast. He was deadly pale, and the eyes were closed—and, moreover, the weight in the arms of the father told him that his son had heard him not.

With a cry of alarm, Belmont bore him to the sofa, and sprung to the bell, which he violently pulled. A terrible idea that he might be dead, for a moment nearly crazed the man. But the boy had only fainted from the sudden surprise acting upon a constitution enfeebled by nights of wakefulness and days of undermining excitement.

CHAPTER XIV.

IT was not long before the medical assistance
summoned by Belmont restored the boy to consciousness, and on that same afternoon the two
drove off to the Hôtel de la Grande Bretagne,
where, it will be remembered, Belmont had given
his address to M. Malherbe.

The excitement having now in a measure
passed away, the father was enabled to contemplate with more calmness the extraordinary series
of events that had concluded at once in destroy-
ing his two foes and in restoring to him his son.

How many years in the solitude of the cell,
in the degradation of punishment, in the wilds of
an uncivilised country, or in the populous city of
a distant land, this man may have employed in the
meditation of his scheme of revenge upon the de-
stroyers of all that he held most sacred in the
world—no human tongue can now declare. Nor

can it be known whether he returned to his native land with a design of vengeance in his head which circumstances of a nature more conducive to the attainment of his end interrupted and replaced. But never in the history of our nature's sweetest but most unholy passion, Revenge, was it forwarded by the hand of chance with such a succession of almost startling coincidences as in the present instance. It would seem as if Fate had herself grasped the scheme, and fitted each part to the other with an accuracy that had left the invention of Belmont nothing to supply. The infirmity of one was adapted to the powers of another—this weakness was proportioned to that strength; this overreaching ambition of vice to that undermining cunning of malignancy. Even to one less superstitious than Belmont, the thought might have occurred of a supernatural intervention in the order of things, smoothing every obstruction away from the progress of him whose destiny was retribution, whose mission was revenge.

But for the discovery of his son, life would have had nothing more to offer him. His end had been accomplished, and nothing now remained but to return to England, and to lay himself down in the slumber of death by the side of his long lost wife.

But the presence of his boy awoke in him a new existence; there was something now to live for, and henceforth he was not to be desolate and alone. Yet even this joy was mingled with a bitterness that bade fair to sap the foundations of that airy fabric of joy which seemed to have reared itself by enchantment before him. Could the father tell his son that he had been a convict? Would the disclosure of the infernal plot of his two dead foes mitigate the horror with which the boy would but too surely contemplate this slur upon his father's character? The fact was not to be dismissed. Dishonour could not be forgotten. Sympathy and generosity might compel the son into silence; but in his heart would dwell the recollection of the father's avowal, clogging his feet, perhaps, in the hour of ambitious action, and turning him from the attainment of honour and position by the dread of ridicule, the fear of contempt, the memory of shame!

A terrible struggle was taking place in the heart of the father as all these thoughts rushed across him. One moment he was determined to confess all to his son—tell him that the finger of Wrong had marked him out as her victim, all innocent as he was—noble-minded as he had ever been. The next, he was resolved to maintain silence; peacefully to secure the happiness of his child, and when he had placed him in the possession of every gratification that he could confer, to leave him silently, and from some remote land reveal to him the motive of his departure, and to implore him to remember not the misfortunes of his supplicating parent, whose destiny was a dishonour against which he had been powerless to contend.

The father and the son remained together the whole evening, extending their conversation into a late hour of the night. Several times had Belmont been on the point of confessing the stain upon his character; but a strange dread sealed his lips, and the hours wore away, and the disclosure came not.

The son was full of Rosalie. He wanted to seek her out at once, and at her feet pour out, too, *his* confession, which was no less torturing than his father's. He acquainted Belmont with his love; told him how he had known her as a little child; how her lips were the first that had ever opened to him with words of kindness—yet, as he spoke, he remembered the old father whom his crime had killed, and bowing his head in his hands, he gave way to a violent burst of emotion.

The father was strangely touched at his son's distress, and strove to comfort him.

"Fear not," he said; "if she loves you, she will pity and pardon. This is the prerogative of love, and true love always exerts it. In the morning, seek her out; bring her to me. I will converse with her. Tell her to look upon me as her father. If she be worthy of you, or you of her, my sanction alone can be wanting to the marriage, and that you have. If not, I will make some provision for her, that shall compensate in a measure the suffering she must have endured."

"I have but one request to make you," said the young man, looking up at his father, "and that is, that you will place her in a convent or with some family until I can afford to marry her. Now I am a beggar, and I love her too fondly to unite her to poverty."

The father glanced at him with a look of compassion, but made no reply.

Early the next morning, Williams—I will continue to call him so—rose, after a troubled night, and dressing himself with care, made a hasty breakfast, and left the hotel. His father had not yet risen, and he would not disturb him. He walked rapidly along the streets in the direction of the Rue Colville, his heart sinking within him at each step that brought him nearer to his destination.

The morning was bright and almost cloudless. The streets were full of people speeding to their houses of business, and the cheerful appearance of the city, the laughing conversation of the light-hearted persons passing him, the whistling of *gamins*, and the noise of the passing vehicles, served in a measure to lighten the heart of the young man of the gloom of depression that had settled upon it. But after passing the busy thoroughfares, he emerged into the more silent *quartier* of the city in which he had resided, and here he again grew uneasy and nervous.

The sight of the Rue Colville restored to him all the feelings of bitterness with which he now associated the place. He passed the corner of a street, where only two nights before he had flown by, a thief and—haply ignorant of it then—a murderer. How high the wind was then! how bleak and desolate the night! how cold, too, he had felt in his wet clothes, through which the wind had penetrated to his very bones!

Before turning the corner he stopped and pressed his hand over his eyes. A sudden terror took possession of him, and he feared each moment the contact of a heavy hand upon his shoulder, arresting him for robbery and murder. Subduing his emotion with a violent effort, he pressed forward and entered the Rue Colville.

A murmur of despair escaped his lips as the first thing that his eyes encountered was a hearse standing half-way up the street, and opposite, as he knew, to M. Gautier's house. A lurking hope which he had attempted wholly to stifle, that the news of M. Gautier's death was not true, had been with him. But with this spectacle before him the fact was made terribly certain.

As he stood watching this, a cab drove up to the door; and a few minutes after a young girl, enveloped in a black veil, came out of the house and entered it. At the same moment the driver mounted the one-horse hearse, and the two vehicles proceeded to move away.

Pulling his hat over his brows, and keeping his head in a bent posture, Williams quickened his steps, and in a short while had approached to within forty or fifty yards of the last carriage. Then adopting the same pace as them, he proceeded to follow them.

Though he had barely glanced at M. Gautier's house as he passed, he had noticed that the shutters were all closed, and that those belonging to the office-window still bore the marks of the insertion of the iron bar. More than this he dared not view.

The hearse took the direction of the great cemetery, Père la Chaise, which lay in a direction west of the position the mourners then occupied. It was a long walk for the young man, and once or twice he thought of approaching the carriage in which he knew Rosalie to be seated alone; but the windows were both up, and a dread that amounted almost to a terror of intruding upon the rapt grief of the young girl—a grief of which he himself was the cause—restrained him.

M. Gautier had died a Protestant, and a grave dug in that part of the cemetery devoted to dissenting creeds awaited him. An English minister stood by the spot, and presently the coffin, borne on the shoulders of four men, and followed by the figure of a girl clothed in black—the only mourner !—came along the gravel walk, and approached the prepared resting-place.

Gliding in after them, the young man posted himself behind a tall grave-stone, and in an attitude of profound melancholy remained a silent spectator of the scene.

The funeral service was soon performed, and the minister, addressing a few words of consolation to the weeping girl, walked away. The earth was thrown upon the coffin, the little mound piled, and the sexton, with a look of compassion at the young mourner, whose head was bowed upon her breast, trod noiselessly in the same direction that had been pursued by the clergyman.

When the girl found herself alone, she knelt down by the side of the new grave, and clasping her hands over her face, bent herself in the attitude of prayer. The consciousness that he himself was the cause of this bereaved woman's despair, smote upon the heart of Williams with redoubled force. He flung himself down by the side of the grave-stone against which he had been leaning, and burying his face in his hands sobbed aloud.

This outburst of passion seemed after a while to relieve him: for he raised his head and looked in the direction of Rosalie. She had risen from her devout attitude, and was standing with clasped hands and eyes fixed upon the fresh turf—the purest embodiment of musing Desolation.

Rising to his feet he made a movement towards her, and then paused and pressed his hand to his heart. At this moment, perhaps hearing his foot-step, Rosalie looked up, and recognising him in an instant, she extended her hands towards him.

With bowed head and trembling steps he timidly advanced, and without accepting the prof-fered hand of the girl, flung himself down upon the grave of her parent, striking his forehead upon the yielding earth, and remaining mo-tionless with clenched hands outspread before him.

Attributing his distress to sympathy with her bereavement, she bent over him and laid a trem-bling hand upon his shoulder. " I thank you for your sympathy," she murmured; "the blow is terrible, but do not let it afflict you so much, for my sake."

He remained without answering her for some time in the prostrate position he had assumed: then, slowly staggering to his feet, he stood trembling before her, his face haggard, his eyes red with weeping, his whole aspect telling of his acute distress.

"You do not take my hand," she murmured, in her low, sweet voice, again proffering it to him, "you are my only friend now, and are you going to desert me?"

"Desert you!" He grasped the little hand, and bringing it rapidly to his lips imprinted upon it a long, passionate kiss. Then he suddenly let it fall.

"Rosalie!" he said mournfully. "By the grave of your lost father I have come to bid you farewell for ever. His presence sanctifies the adieu — but his death separates us in this world."

He could not see her features, but through her veil he beheld her large eyes fixed upon him with a sad, earnest gaze.

"And why are you going to leave me?" she asked, in a trembling voice.

There was a long pause. The young man's fingers were nervously twisting themselves about, and he seemed as if he were about to burst out into a wild fit of laughter—so strange, so terrible, was the expression of his face.

"You ask me why I am going to leave you?"

he said, bending his body and approaching her by a step. "I will tell you: because I am *your father's murderer!*"

Rosalie uttered a cry and spread her hands out before her with a gesture of horror.

"Leave me!" he cried aloud, raising his hands above his head, as if he were deprecating the wrath of the skies; "loathe me! shrink from my presence, and think the very atmosphere I breathe polluted by my breath! I am not worthy to remain a moment longer in your sight. If you knew me as I know myself, you would bid me never again enter your presence!" and he flung himself prostrate before the girl.

She was alarmed by his frenzy; but her fear was only momentary. Stooping down she gently assisted him to rise, and led him tenderly to a flat tombstone a few paces away, upon which she seated him. Then anxiously looking at him she said, "Tell me, why do you accuse yourself of this? It may be your fancy; my poor father was not murdered."

He struck himself upon the breast as he answered, "Yes, I tell you I am his murderer."

"Were you the——" a sudden terror stifled the remainder of the sentence, and throwing up her veil she fixed her eyes with an alarmed, despairing look on the face of her lover. He bowed his head and she comprehended the gesture; for she turned her face away and covered it with her hands.

He grasped her by the arm and strove to speak. Several times his voice failed him; at length in a hoarse, broken whisper he said, "Do not look away from me—it will break my heart! do not hide your face, or I shall think that you really loathe me! Speak to me—encourage me by a look! I am guilty; but it was want—beggary. Rosalie, you, *you* were, too, the cause of this act! I loved you, Rosalie; I was poor—I could not wed you to poverty, and I sought in a gambling-house to augment the means that I sighed to lay at your feet, and cry, 'Let me win you now!' Do not turn from me! I am a villain! but could I have foreseen the death of this good old man, I would have died ere a single thought to—to—to —" he dared not speak the word rob, but gulping down a long breath he went on: "I should have repaid him, Rosalie. Ay, twenty-fold should his money have been returned to him. It was for you, darling of my heart, that I was tempted to commit this crime. Will you not look upon me? Oh, this, this is bitterness!"

Slowly she brought her eyes to look upon him; they were red with the silent tears that had flowed during his wild speech, and her lips were quivering with the emotion she strove in vain to suppress.

"I will not upbraid you," she murmured. "He might have lent you the money; he was not cruel-hearted. He was frightened, and—and—died! Oh, my father!" again she turned her head away, this time to conceal the flood of tears that suddenly burst from her eyes.

The young man threw himself at her feet.

"Mercy, mercy!" he cried; "I have wronged you, Rosalie, I will leave you! But have mercy upon me—forgive me—pity me! You knew not the temptation—ah, I could say so much, but words are useless. Give me your forgiveness—I will trouble you no more! I will leave you— perhaps to die—but grant me your forgiveness. Have I it?"

He looked at her despairingly; she slowly turned her head, until her eyes met his.

"You have it," she murmured.

He kissed her hand wildly, and exclaimed, "Rosalie, I will leave you. It will break my heart; but how could you suffer in your presence

a criminal—a murderer—the murderer of your
father! Yet I loved you, Rosalie—passionately
did I love you! I would have given my heart's
best blood for you; ay, for you, I have brought
myself to this! But I am a murderer," he continued shudderingly. "You must loathe me.
The sight of that grave must ever awaken in your
heart—oh! what thoughts of me! But I have
your forgiveness! I am happy—I did not think
to win it. Rosalie, my love, my own, farewell!
Remember me not with scorn! I erred for you,
and——"

He struck his clenched fist against his forehead,
and rose to his feet. Then burying his face in his
hands, he moved slowly away.

She sat gazing after him, speechless, motionless—with a yearning in her heart to call him
back, and yet with a tongue that refused to give
utterance to the syllable. Was she going to lose
him, then, for ever? Would he never more
return to her? She loved him; oh, how fondly!
yet he was departing from her, to return to her
no more; and she called him not back. Alone—
she was alone now, indeed! No father, no lover,
no friend. Ah, it was terrible! A look of
despair swept over the face of the poor girl, and

she extended her arms towards the receding form of her lover, as if to woo him back to her by the mute appeal of that eloquent gesture.

As she did so, he turned his head towards her, perhaps to take one lingering look at all that he held most dear, most cherished on earth. Beholding her arms extended towards him, he started and stopped. For the moment, he might have doubted his eye-sight, as he hesitated to return; but no, he was not mistaken — not dreaming, and with a cry of joy he sprang to her side, and clasped her to his heart.

Silently they remained for some moments in this attitude, until he almost thought she must have fainted, so motionless had she become.

When she raised her eyes to his, they were heavy with tears, but their expression told of content, peace, perhaps happiness.

"And you have forgiven me?" he murmured.

She threw a look of devotion to the skies, and then pointing to her father's grave, she whispered, "And so would he, could he see us now."

"Darling, you are mine now. You have lost a father, but you have won a husband. Ah, if perfect love, if the adoration of a life-time can expiate my terrible offence, let it be erased from your memory, for my heart is yours."

Again she pointed to her father's grave, as she answered,—

"Let the recollection sleep with him. In life, we shall know it no more; in death, if it is to be remembered, God is just: He is the only one wronged, and He is merciful."

He pressed her to his heart, and then drawing her arm through his, gently led her away.

In silence they passed through the sacred habitations of the dead, and not until they stood without the cemetery did he venture to address her. Then he said,—

"Rosalie, since we met, many strange things have taken place. But one is so extraordinary— so unexpected, that in spite of my feeling it to be the truth, I can hardly believe it to be real."

She turned her quiet eyes up to his, as she asked him what it was.

"I have found my father, Rosalie!"

She started, and pressing his arm, said,—

"Strange, indeed! Yet I am not surprised, for I fancied it would come to pass."

"Yes, I have found him, and in this extraordinary manner. But the story is long. I will call a fly, and hasten to introduce you to him. He is at the Hôtel de la Grande Bretagne, and—and Rosalie," he said in a whisper, "he has given me his sanction for our marriage."

She blushed, and another pressure of his arm was her reply.

But he had suddenly grown grave, and his voice wore a sad tone.

"Alas," he said, "though he has sanctioned our marriage, I am poor. Poor? I am a very beggar, and to ally myself to you as I am, would be to bring you to misery."

She blushed and hesitated a little, and then timidly glancing at him, she whispered,—

"I have a little money ; poor papa did not die a beggar."

"That is true—ah ! Perhaps my father will make me a little allowance, which, united to your store, will enable us to begin life. I am young, and can do many things."

There was a pause, and when he looked at her he found her to be weeping.

"Dry your tears, my darling," he whispered ; "you must not weep now."

"Ah," she murmured, "you find your father just as I lose mine. He was a good father to me.

Let me cry; my tears are all that I can offer to his memory now."

Williams' heart was full; he could have mingled his tears with hers, but with a violent effort he succeeded in subduing his emotion.

Calling a *cabriolet*, he handed Rosalie into it, and, bidding the coachman drive to the hotel, seated himself by the side of his betrothed.

During the ride, he communicated to her, just as he had communicated to Belmont, the whole narrative of his life, since his first meeting with her in the stationer's shop. She listened to him with a terrified countenance, when he told her of his first visit to the Rue Antoine Sarbotière; and with sympathetic tears, when he related his temptations, his privations, his sufferings, and his final flight. But when he came to the transactions at "La Maison Rouge," the spectacle of the two dead bodies that had greeted his sight on entering the room, she shuddered with horror, and buried her face in his breast, as if to hide the hideous picture he had placed so palpably before her. Whether, owing to her very warm prejudice in his favour, or whether to the unvarnished narrative that he poured into her ears, it is certain that when he had concluded, every feeling save pity and compassion for her lover's meditated crime and its result, had vanished from her gentle heart. Indeed, she began to think that—what with the society of Sloman, what with the seductions of the gambling-house, what with the prospects of the future—so utterly dark, unless irradiated by some created hope—and what with the concentrated incitement of the whole to urge him on to a deed of iniquity—even men of far greater experience of life than Williams, of virtues far more solid, because far more cultivated, would have fallen ; and perhaps into an error or a crime far more iniquitous than that meditated by her lover.

And for the sake of my young hero, I heartily hope that my kind-hearted reader, whose broad survey of human manners and life has made him indulgent towards the failings and shortcomings of human nature, will join with Rosalie in her pitying and benevolent belief.

But now the carriage had drawn up at the door of the hotel, and handing Rosalie out, Williams bade the porter pay the cabman his fare. He could not help wondering, now that the moment had arrived, how his father would welcome Rosalie, and what impression she would make upon him.

"Is Mr. Belmont in?" he demanded.

"Just this moment entered, sir."

"Where is he?"

"In his sitting-room, up-stairs, sir, I believe."

Giving his arm to Rosalie, he conducted her to the private apartment which he and his father had occupied the preceding night. Rapping at the door, Belmont's voice cried, "Come in," and he entered.

The moment his father caught sight of him, he rose from his chair, and coming forward in an agitated manner, he exclaimed,—

"Why, where have you been? Your absence greatly alarmed me." But seeing Rosalie, his voice fell, and he murmured, "Ah, now I comprehend."

"This is Rosalie Gautier," said Williams; "and Rosalie, this is my father."

There seemed something so strange in the word "father" to the young man, that his voice faltered as he spoke it, and he turned to see the effect of it upon him to whom he had applied the word.

But Belmont had seized Rosalie by the hand, and, gracefully bowing, conducted her to a chair.

"I suppose," he said, "my son has acquainted

you with the particulars of our extraordinary meeting, Mademoiselle Rosalie?"

"Yes," said Rosalie, glancing lovingly at Williams. "Ah, poor boy. I am sure he wants a father; he has been a long time alone in the world." And she sighed.

Belmont noticed her mourning garments, and remembered her late bereavement. Tenderly raising her hand, and pressing it between both of his, he exclaimed, "Condolence from a stranger is but a poor remedy for grief; but you must suffer me to express to you how deeply I sympathise with you in your late loss. We have all our sufferings to undergo, and happy are they who can submit to them with resignation. May he," pointing to his son, "only prove as good a husband to you, as you have proved a good daughter to him whom heaven has removed from a cold and selfish world." And he imprinted a paternal kiss upon her hand with a gesture full of love and reverence.

Her tears had again commenced to flow; but there was less of sorrow in them now than before. The grandeur and refined bearing of Belmont had won the young girl's heart at once. Almost secluded as she had been by her father's profession, which, in a measure, had prohibited her from social intercourse, the noble-looking man before her impressed her with a double sense of his superiority; and in spite of his age, and in spite of her love, she was divided in her opinion as to the appearance of the father and the son; her woman's heart owning its preference to the impulsive character and haughty manners of the younger, whilst her maidenly feelings sought refuge in the stately bearing and impressive yet fatherly aspect of the elder.

"May I call you Rosalie?" said Belmont.

The young girl faintly smiled, and said yes.

"Rosalie will, of course, take up her abode with us now," said Belmont, turning to his son; "have you concerted your arrangements between you?" he added, smiling.

Williams slightly blushed and stammered, as he said,—

"We are—both poor—and Rosalie——"

"Well?"

"In a word, I am about to throw myself on your generosity," exclaimed the young man, seizing his father's hand. "I cannot marry Rosalie yet, for I am too poor. But I am young, and, incited by claiming her when my task is accomplished, I will set to work with a will, and strive to acquire enough to render me capable of taking her to my heart. Meanwhile, I am going to solicit your exertion to place her in a family or a convent, until I am ready to call her wife. And until then," he added, glancing sadly at Rosalie, " we must wait."

Mr. Belmont watched him for a few moments in silence; a slight smile full of gentleness and love played over the haughty mouth. Turning to Rosalie, he exclaimed,—

" And what do you say?"

Rosalie's face wore a sad, but firm expression. Pointing to her lover, she answered—

" I am ready to do whatever he wishes. As he says, we are poor; but I have a—little—money "—here she hesitated—" left me by my poor father, and we thought——"

" You thought what, Rosalie?"

She glanced timidly at her lover, as she answered,—

" We thought that if you could add a little to it we might be enabled to commence life, for Frederick could always be making more."

Belmont made no reply. For some moments he appeared to be lost in thought. Then he placed himself before the lovers—the benefactor and the father, eager for their happiness and mindless of his own.

"I have found you, my son," he said, "after many years of suffering to us both. You have asked me for my history, and you shall have it soon. I know you have suffered much in the few years that you have lived in this world; and if any proof were wanting to confirm the truth of your story, it would be made known to me by the fact that a son of *mine* has stooped to degradation and dishonour to supply those wants which Nature gave, but to which men refused to minister. It is time that you were happy— that we were both happy; for we have both suffered. I am rich; therefore the only obstacle that prevents you uniting yourself to Rosalie is removed. My wealth is yours—take it all, and leave me only enough to subsist upon. Had I not have discovered you, there would have been nothing now for me to live for; but—but——" He paused and clasped his hand to his forehead, and then continued, in a low, soft voice,—"It is a joy for me to know that I can minister, it matters not how, to the happiness of you both. It is sufficient for me that you are my son—and or her, that she is your betrothed. Your claims upon me are equal. Nothing now need prevent your marriage. I have already given you my sanction. Your future happiness lies with yourselves."

He seated himself in his chair, and gazed at them from eyes beaming with benevolence and goodness.

In an instant, his son was at his feet, pouring out to him his thanks in glowing language. Rosalie had also risen, and was standing by his side, one arm round his neck, and her hand locked in his.

Suddenly, a dark look of anxiety swept across Belmont's face, and disengaging himself from the grasp of the young couple, he rose to his feet. The hour had come when he was to reveal himself to his son, to pronounce himself a convict—in a word, to narrate the history of his life.

" Rosalie," he said, mournfully, turning to her, for the dread upon his heart as to the way in which his son would receive his communication was great; " Rosalie, I have something to impart to my son in confidence. Will you think us rude if we leave you alone for a short while ? We will not keep you long; and some of these days the revelation I am about to communicate to my son shall be made known to you."

Then, taking his son by the arm, he led him into an adjoining room, and closed the door.

For a long while, Rosalie remained alone. She heard constantly the humming tones of Belmont's voice, interrupted once only by a sudden exclamation from the lips of her lover, uttered in a voice expressive of horror and passion. It was a weary time for the poor girl, as her thoughts reverted to her dead father, and with them her tears commenced to flow anew. But the future stood before, bright and happy, and gradually her feelings took a calmer mood, and a sense of rest and peace and almost happiness came over her.

At last the door opened and Belmont came out, followed by his son. A smile was upon the father's face, and his whole countenance was lighted up with an expression of grandeur and repose that lent his handsome features a new beauty. Frederick went over to Rosalie, and taking both her hands, murmured in her ear,—

"Rosalie, we live in a strange world—be surprised at nothing."

What had passed between the father and the son, the reader has of course conjectured.

"Henceforth," said Belmont to Rosalie, "your betrothed's name will be Hamilton—Frederick Hamilton; and mine, Frank Hamilton."

Rosalie again looked at her lover with surprise, but made no remark.

"To-morrow," continued Hamilton, "shall be a busy day with us. The inquest on the bodies of Sloman and Murray will occupy the morning; and the afternoon," he said, addressing Rosalie, "we will devote to an examination of your poor father's affairs, and then, children, we will return to England." He paused, and then continued, "You can well dispense with my society for a short while. I know what young lovers are, for, Rosalie, I have loved myself."

He withdrew himself from the apartment, and entered the room in which he had held the conference with his son.

He stood for a short while with his face bowed in his hands. The hot tears came trickling through his fingers, and his breast heaved as with some inward agitation. In that short moment his whole past life rose up before him; like the drowning man, who, lying prone upon the pebbly floor of a river, perceives clearly around him the vision of some golden happiness almost forgotten in the years gone by; so this man, raising his head, and stretching forth his hands, with a smile of ineffable grandeur upon his face, seemed to draw to his heart the phantom of some old delight that stood before him; then, raising his hands to heaven, with a look of supreme devotion, he breathed forth the one word, " Eveleen," and he fell upon his knees beside a chair, and bowed himself in prayer.

So let him remain, whilst we let the curtain gently fall upon a scene that belongs not to this record.

CONCLUSION.

As with the dramatist, so is it with the novelist. The play must conclude with an assemblage of the principal personages who have been concerned in its action; and no novel can be called completed whose final chapter leaves in doubt the fate of those who have been employed in the conduct of the story.

In obedience, therefore, to a custom venerable by its antiquity, a few words shall be devoted to those characters in these volumes in whom my reader may have felt sufficient interest to care to know their ultimate lot.

In a charming little house on the banks of the Thames, and close to Henley, dwelt Mr. Hamilton and his wife Rosalie; and with them Mr. Hamilton, *père*. It had been partly to gratify his father that the young man had selected this spot for his residence; for the grave of Eveleen, the Wife and Mother, was near them: and to her tomb the father would pay long and frequent visits. He had become a reserved and silent man, seeing no society but his son and his daughter-in-law, and amusing himself the greater part of the day with rambles about the country, or in a small boat which he had constructed, and in which he would often row himself into some shady nook, and alone and in silence dream away the hours. Rosalie had frequently petitioned her husband to tell her of the past life of his father, and one day he did so, having first of all gained permission. She listened with rapt attention to the singular narrative, and felt incredulous as to its truth, so amazing did the whole appear, and so much like the plot of some improbable romance. Indeed, it was not easy for this girl to understand how a man could so long endure his wrongs, buoyed up only by the hopes of revenge, which after all might never have been realised. She could not conceive it possible that a convict should find his way up into the wilds of Australia; there, by unflagging industry, realise a sufficient competence; embark for Hongkong, and before his departure, learn the death of his wife from a newspaper: a piece of information that determined him yet to prosecute his scheme of acquiring greater wealth in order with more certainty to wreak his vengeance upon his enemies when he should return to England; to proceed to Hongkong, and there, by his diligence, secure himself a partnership in a house of excellent position; and when fancying he had sufficient means, to sell his share in the concern, and to retrace his steps back to his native land, solely incited by the hopes of vengeance on those from whom he had been separated for years, and who might have been long since dead—for aught he could tell.

And the improbability seemed greater when she contemplated this strange being, who, after his extraordinary career, could so quietly settle down by the banks of an English river, occupying himself in the most inoffensive pastimes, equipped in an old coat, a large straw hat, and a stout walking-stick! But the stolid reiteration of her husband's assertions as to the authenticity of his father's history at length prevailed: and a belief in its probability dawned at length upon her, and gradually grew into a conviction. In process of time Rosalie presented a little child to the delighted husband; and when the boy grew old enough, he became the constant companion of his grandfather. So in peace this little family lived: and peace they merited; for they had all three seen much suffering in their lives.

* * * * * * *

The fate of Mr. Jerkins is involved in obscurity: the only information that I have succeeded in gaining of him being a dark tradition that he had taken to drinking, and to beating his wife; that his business, from his dissolute habits, had gradually melted away: his connexion having deserted him for many reasons, amongst which may be enumerated certain extravagant charges for articles of under-clothing which, when examined, were found to be worth only a fractional part of the money that had been paid for them; that for one night and a whole week after, he was missing; that his wife had inquiries instituted for him, but that nothing was found but a coat-tail which was recognised as belonging to him by a singular brass button attached to it, an ornament with which he delighted to render himself remarkable; that his disconsolate wife was one day found missing too; and that the sons finding themselves bereft of home, food, and shelter, migrated to remote lands, some as sailors, some as soldiers, and one as a felon. The same dark tradition, however, adds that Mrs. Jerkins was one day met by an old acquaintance in the streets of London, bearing upon her head a large basket of oranges, as a vendor of which article of metropolitan consumption, the acquaintance presumed that she supported life. It may be useful to the speculator on the mutability of human affections to know that this same acquaintance, in spite of Mrs. Jerkins' smile of recognition, glared at her full in the face, and passed by her with stolid contempt.

A few west-end drawing-rooms, of which the possessors are City men eager for society, are occasionally honoured by the presence of a fat, smiling, and pretty woman, who generally makes her appearance alone, and whose dancing, flirtations, and forward manners, are the invariable provocatives of much remark and a great deal of scandal. The husband, whom Rumour asserts to have been once a well-disposed young man, has become dissipated and discontented: gratifying his discontent by such balm as clubs, whist, a little hunting, and much smoking, can supply.

The reader will hardly be surprised to learn that these persons are Mr. Frank Collins and his wife, formerly Miss Alice Lloyd. That the former should have taken the trouble to gain for himself a character so little pleasing, all must regret; but the lady had held out in her younger days the promise of her future career. It only adds one more justification to the truth of the Irish sentiment: That he who has a mind to unite himself to a flirt, had better first drown himself and then marry her afterwards.

The honest game-keeper, his wife and child, still live. The first has become a florist: the second buxom and fat in the face: and the last, a sturdy young fellow, who assists his father in training plants, and preparing bouquets. Time has not impaired their pleasant recollection of the little boy Freddy; and should it ever be their fate to encounter him, the meeting will be no less delightful because they discover the stripling of ten to have expanded into the man of three-and-twenty, with a wife and family.

Of the remaining men and women whose names adorn these pages, some are dead, and some are yet alive. The town of Y—— has long since been absorbed in the avaricious grasp of

England's metropolis. It boasts its market-days no more; the house in which the business of the United British Banking Company was transacted has been pulled down, together with the butcher's shop at its side, to make way for an extension of the premises of the Baptists' meeting-house. The only memorial that stands as a guarantee of Y——'s former isolation and independence, is the ivy-covered church and rectory, once the living of the Rev. James Smallands.

THE END.

BRADBURY, EVANS, AND CO., PRINTERS, WHITEFRIARS.

"THE ARGOSY."

EDITED BY

MRS. HENRY WOOD,

AUTHOR OF "EAST LYNNE," "THE CHANNINGS," ETC. ETC.

This Magazine of light and choice reading will, from the commencement of the new volume, be conducted by the Author of "East Lynne," and will be published by Charles W. Wood, 13, Tavistock Street, Strand.

The December number will commence the new volume. It will contain the opening chapters of a new three-volume story by the Author of "East Lynne," a story by Hesba Stretton, and various other papers.

Price Sixpence Monthly.